D1758026

Roger Pulvers is an author, playwright, theatre director, translator and filmmaker. He has published more than 50 books in Japanese and English, including novels, essays, plays, and poetry. Working as assistant to director Nagisa Oshima on "*Merry Christmas, Mr. Lawrence*" and befriending David Bowie brought him back to Japan and inspired him to become the award-winning playwright, film director and prolific author he is today. His most recent novel, *Hoshizuna Monogatari* (*Star Sand*), which he wrote in Japanese, was published by Kodansha, Japan's largest publisher, in 2015 and subsequently in English and French in 2016 and 2017 respectively. It was released as a film, directed by him, in 2017.

Roger Pulvers

LIV

A Novel

Balestier Press
London · Singapore

Balestier Press
71-75 Shelton Street, London WC2H 9JQ
www.balestier.com

LIV
Copyright © Roger Pulvers, 2018

First published by Balestier Press in 2018

A CIP catalogue record for this book
is available from the British Library.

ISBN 978 1 911221 27 2

Cover illustration by Lucy Pulvers

All rights reserved. No part of this publication may be reproduced, stored in a retrieval system or transmitted in any form or by any means, electronic, mechanical, without the prior written permission of the publisher of this book.

This book is a work of fiction. The literary perceptions and insights are based on experience, all names, characters, places, and incidents either are products of the author's imagination or are used fictitiously.

LIV

I HAD LIVED my life up to then believing that whatever degree of evil I encountered in the world I would never perpetrate an act of evil of my own.

I was single and childless. I had turned fifty-five on May 4th of that year, 1975, and in the eyes of others—if not my own—I did believe that I had done admirable things within my small power to help people survive desperate circumstances. There was a time, when I was twenty-five, that I had found myself in just such circumstances. I had been certain that I would not survive them. But the chaotic cruelty and permanent misery striking those around me had somehow brushed by me ... passed me by. The fire in the building I was working in had left me unscathed and, I had long thought, unscarred. The loss I had suffered at the hands of others—particularly one other—was borne. The sinister net surrounding me had somehow come undone, its very ropes offering me a means of escape, allowing me to scurry away while everyone and everything around me was seemingly being trapped in it.

I took myself far away from the edge of what had turned into an abyss. I was determined never to let the depraved instincts of people—the flak of the past—reach me again.

The nave of the disused church at Cabramatta was like the deck of a ship; the pews lined against the walls, its railing. The Vietnamese who had found refuge there had all come to Australia by air. Now they were on this safe and stable deck, resting, eating, conversing … preparing themselves to walk freely out into the scorching Australian sun.

I was spending three days a week as a volunteer for refugees in this suburb some thirty kilometres from the centre of Sydney, serving food, comforting crying infants and gathering dirty clothes to take down to the washing machines in the basement. On this particular day, Tuesday, 7 October 1975, I noticed a little girl. She looked to be age ten, standing by herself, leaning against the jarrah wood lectern and peering vacantly over the heads of the others.

"MINAKO!" My eyes shut tightly, as if a rough hand was forcing my lids down. I clamped my nostrils with my thumb and forefinger to prevent the stench of smoke from sickening me. I coughed from the smoke and tried not to breathe.

The Vietnamese girl was still there when I managed to open my eyes and gradually return to the present. She was looking directly at me across the church's nave. Yet even with my eyes open, the past was continuing to return in flashes. Minako had been standing in the corridor outside my room in the embassy. Flames shooting out of a metal box spilled onto her as if they were a liquid, setting her light-green dress alight. I spread my body over her, smothering the flames.

Minako's prostrate body rocked in my embrace.

"She is telling you to let go of her. Please let go of her."

I stared into the little Vietnamese girl's face. She was breathing heavily and weeping. An aid worker stood above me.

"Oh, I am so sorry," I said, dropping my hands to my sides. "I don't know what came over me."

"You rushed across the hall and threw yourself at this girl," said the aid worker. "Are you all right?"

I left the church earlier than usual. The memory of Minako's dress catching fire at the embassy in May 1945—a memory that had not disturbed my thoughts a single time since coming to live in Australia—had unsettled me. Perhaps it was the force of this memory, bringing with it the stench of smoke, that prompted me to think the Vietnamese girl was Minako and that she would recognize me when I knelt in front of her.

Then on the train going home, as if to stir those dormant scraps of ash and rekindle them, another memory returned to me, despite the force of will of thirty years to keep that ash cold. It came in the form not of a stench or a spark or a flame but of a glare in the man's cornflower-blue eyes, those terrifying vengeful malicious piercing eyes that were saying to me softly but insistently, "Liv, you will never escape me!"

He came onto the train at Roseville and sat directly opposite me. He carried a stick, which he propped against the seat. He stared straight at me. Those very same eyes, that very same blinding flash in them, two knives extending outward until their steel points were about to penetrate my irises!

I had to look away. But I continued to observe him out of the corner of my eye where my vision is sharpest. His other features did not match those of *that man*. The bridge of his nose was wider; the lips, fuller; the ears, pinned back against the scalp rather than protruding. He did not resemble that man save for those blade-like eyes. As the train began to slow down for its stop at Killara, he stood, knocking his stick to the ground. I bolted up, reaching out for it. I picked up the stick and proffered it to him with its polished and worn silver knob angled towards his open palm.

"Thank you very much," he said, grasping the knob and

tilting his head to one side.

The doors opened and he left the train. I watched him as he walked laboriously, using his stick, towards the stairs. I did not take my eyes off his back. The train was pulling away as he rounded the top of the stairs and disappeared.

He had an accent, I thought, but his voice was too soft to detect the kind of accent. That man always did speak softly. It made his words all the more cutting and venomous. Their poison had seeped into me from the cuts. I had convinced myself that no trace of it, not so much as a needle-thin scar, was left on my skin or in my mind. But seeing the cornflower-blue eyes of the man on the train, and feeling their gaze's pointed ends, changed everything. The scar was still there, ready to open up, the poison was still inside me, deep inside me … and there seemed like no normal way to arrest its flow or rid myself of its consequences.

I had arrived in Australia at the beginning of 1956 from Norway, age thirty-five. Though Norway was "my" country, I had never lived there before the war. My parents had been missionaries in the small southern Japanese port town of Moji. They died there of typhoid fever in November 1939 within days of each other, leaving me alone and stranded. They had kept making trips to villages in the mountains of Oita and as far away as Miyazaki and Kagoshima. Many people in those remote villages were desperate and starving. The young men were already leaving for China, with only children, young women and old people left to plant and harvest the rice. My parents died of exhaustion for God. Looking back, it often occurred to me that they had loved God more than they had cared for me.

I fended for myself, thanks to help and charity from my parents' Japanese parishioners. After Norway was occupied by Germany, I decided to stay on in Japan; and able to speak fluent Japanese and near-fluent English, I landed a job as translator at the German embassy. Though I could not speak German, I was useful there for being able to translate Japanese documents, many of them obtained secretly, into English so that the ambassador could read them. And so, I moved up to Tokyo in May 1941. But Germany's defeat four years later cast me aside once again, and there seemed nowhere to go in 1946 but "home" to a place that was to me a foreign country—Norway.

I had aspired to what was referred to in postwar Europe as "the quiet life." Yet the polemics of life in Norway were too rash and malicious for my temperament. My countrymen, having to deal with the bitter aftermath of collaboration, required everyone to take a stance, to identify himself and answer the question: What were *you* doing during the war? As for me, I simply wanted to blend in, to be inconspicuous. This did not seem possible in Norway. When asked what I had been doing during the war, all I could say was, "I'd rather not talk about it." I just wished to disappear in my own shadow. Australia was the best place in the world to disappear by starting what people generally refer to as a "new life."

Trade between Australia and Japan had resumed by the mid-1950s, and my skills as a translator of the Japanese language were readily recognized. My passage by ship from Norway to Australia carrying its cargo of Linje Aquavit across the equator seemed to erase every memory of what had transpired in my very ordinary life. "What now, little woman?" I could hear the phrase rattling in my ears. I could hear it through my dreams ... until, by the time all that aquavit and I arrived at Fremantle, Western Australia on 26 January 1956, there was only silence from the past, a wished-for and blessed silence. If this new life for me was to bring only peace, quiet and nothing more, I would welcome it with open arms.

But after being attacked by the fiend's glare in the eyes of *that man*, my new life shattered in an instant like the thin glass over an old photograph, and brittle jagged fragments of my old life tore through my brain. Whatever happened, I could not allow this glare to blind me or the slivers to course through my blood. I would avoid that at all costs. I would strive to be the person I wanted to be, the little person in the poem by Takuboku that I had loved since childhood ...

I continue to disappear into the corner
Of crowded trains.
It's what I admire most about myself.

"This is the life you have always wished for yourself, Liv," I told myself, "sitting in the corner being unnoticed, while others walk by you and get on with their lives. Do not let your life cross with theirs. Stay in the corner, no matter who happens to appear on the train. Do you hear me? This is what you must do, Liv!"

When I returned to Cabramatta two days later I noticed the little girl in the leek-green dress standing on a bench surrounded by several strapping young men. She caught sight of me as I entered the church and jumped off the bench, hiding herself behind the tallest of the young men. She picked up a small suitcase and held it to her chest as if it was a sheet of armour.

I made my way among family groups to the altar where the director, an elderly doctor, was in conversation with two Vietnamese men who had thin moustaches. The doctor turned his head towards me and raised his forefinger as if to say, "Just a moment." The Vietnamese men, evidently not pleased with what they were being told by the doctor, exchanged squint-eyed glances and marched away.

"You are Miss Grimstad, is that right?"

"Yes."

It was late morning. Mothers, grandmothers and daughters

were preparing a variety of simple dishes for lunch on portable gas burners that sat on the floor by the altar.

"I'm Doctor McNaughton."

"Yes, I know."

"I was told about what happened here a couple days ago," he said, looking down at me.

"Did something happen?"

"I was told that you accosted one of the little girls."

"Accosted? Oh dear, I would never in my life do such a thing. I'm …"

"But people saw you rush across the area here and grab her dress."

"Oh. Yes, I did do that. I wasn't thinking."

I threw a glance at the little girl. She was peering at me, still clinging to her suitcase.

"Do you have an explanation for your actions?"

There was no way I could explain why I had rushed towards her, knelt down and embraced her. Had I told the doctor that I had momentarily flashed back to something that had occurred thirty years before then, I would surely have been dismissed from volunteer work and perhaps even been directed to a psychiatrist.

"Well, do you have an explanation? These people here have been traumatized by war. Even the most innocent sudden action can do damage to their mental state. Do you understand that, Miss Grimstad?"

"Oh yes, of course I do. I am so sorry. Should I apologize to her and her family? Would you ask the interpreter to do that for me?"

"That won't be necessary. I think you should just leave. Many of these people here are being transferred out anyway. These are the privileged few, those who had enough money to fly to Australia. The war only ended in April. We are expecting hundreds, if not thousands, of refugees to be coming by boat.

They will be sent from Darwin to places around Australia. Thank you for your assistance, Miss Grimstad. But, if you don't mind my saying it, I do not think you suitable for charitable work."

I stopped off at Central Station to have lunch but spent the time wandering around Chinatown in a daze without eating. I caught the train across the Harbour Bridge in the early afternoon. I could not get the face of the little Vietnamese girl out of my mind. She was staring at me with great fear. Who would fear me? Who could possibly fear someone like me?

And then it happened again. The same man came onto the train at Roseville Station. This time he remained standing by the doors of the car, hooking his stick on the railing at the end of the row of seats. He suddenly swivelled about, looking straight at me. I was now absolutely convinced that he was that man, the most vicious and brutal type of human being imaginable. But how had he survived? How had he been *permitted* to survive?

The train stopped at Lindfield Station. I could see his wrinkled neck and the liver spots on his hands. He must be seventy-five, I thought, perhaps closer to eighty. The age is right.

Martin had said to me …

"I would like nothing more than to wring that neck, that pencil-hack's neck. Why can't I be as brutal as he? I wish I could be, just once. The world might not be a better place, but there would be one less blood-thirsty devil in the little corner of hell that is this embassy."

"You mustn't think like that, Martin. We must just wait. You know as well as I do that Germany will lose this war. Japan will lose as well. You must think only about yourself … and us. He will get what is his due. When the Americans come to Tokyo they will not let him escape."

"Yes, you're right, Liv. You're always right. You are so bright and … and radiant. You light up this pitch-black hellhole. You are my light, Liv. Without you there is no light."

The train had left Lindfield and was slowing down in its approach to Killara. The man lifted his stick off the railing. The train came to a stop, the doors opened and he stepped onto the platform.

"You are so bright and radiant, Liv" … is what Martin had said to me. Could that have been me? Could I have really been like that once? Radiant? Though only fifty-five, I was now a shadow of my old self and I was striving as best as I could to stand in my own shadow, to be unseen in it, not to allow any part of my body to cross over its line and be noticed by others.

I stepped out of the train just before the doors closed, though Killara was not my station. The man was already halfway up the stairs, placing his stick carefully on each step before lifting his leg.

I followed him to nearby Marian St. He did not turn around once. He entered a block of liver-brick flats. I waited several minutes before approaching the block. It had six flats in it. The surnames of the occupants were written beside little white buttons that visitors pressed to announce their arrival.

The names, in order from flat one to six, were …

Greenhalgh
Prowse
Barnes
Miles
Adams
Busby

I took a step back and looked up to the dark balconies with

their thick brick overhangs. Which one belonged to the flat of the man with the stick? How did he get to this place of peace and quiet, to start his little new life after methodically destroying the lives of so many others? Why was he, of all people, allowed to live out his life as he saw fit?

I walked from there all the way to my flat in Gordon. It was strange, but I could see myself clearly on the street that skirted the tracks, as if I was an objective observer. There was purpose in my every step. I had considered myself so benign and full of charity for all. Self-effacing, that's what I was. With me, others came first. But perhaps I wasn't as meek as I saw myself after all. Perhaps I was nothing like the person I saw myself to be. Was my rushing through the nave of the church to embrace the little girl in the leek-green dress a swift journey back to my old self? Whatever I was about to go through, I would not tolerate *that man* dictating the course of events in my present. He had wreaked havoc on my past; and I was determined, on that walk from his home to mine, to prevent him from exercising his will over me ever again.

I took to going to the little park on Marian St. across from his block of flats. Tall eucalyptus trees stood in unevenly spaced rows around an open area with a slide, swings and a picnic table. I sat on a bench attached to the table, spreading out my notebook and two dictionaries. The deadline for the translation of a thick manual for the new Hitachi tape recorder was approaching. I would work on the translation while observing his block of flats. There was no one else at the park except for a young Chinese mother who was carrying her toddler from the bottom of the slide to its ladder over and over again, speaking to him in Cantonese.

An elderly couple, holding hands, emerged from the block of flats across the street. The man sported a navy-blue linen jacket over an open-neck white shirt. The woman wore a pale-blue sleeveless dress with a white cardigan draped over her arm. It was an exceptionally hot spring day. Which flat did this couple live in, I wondered, and what was their name? I ran across the street, leaving my notebook and dictionaries on the picnic table.

"Oh, excuse me," I said, approaching them from behind.

They turned around together, smiling broadly at me.

"Do, um, you by chance live in that block of flats?"

"Yes, we do," said the woman.

"Oh, I was just, I mean, wondering about it because I am moving soon, just from Gordon really, not far, and I love this neighbourhood."

"We love Killara too," she said. "We moved to those flats after our children left home, but we have always lived in Killara. Wouldn't live anywhere else."

"How nice. Um, there wouldn't be a flat in your block empty, or, if not, maybe in the near future, I mean, somebody moving or something?"

"Not that we know of. Is there, Jack?"

The man shook his head.

"Dunno."

"Look, I'm sorry but we must rush," said the woman. "Jack, you rush ahead and buy the tickets."

He gave her a look to say that they should hurry.

"Oh, I'm sorry to keep you," I said.

"That's fine, dear," she said.

She smiled at me and turned towards the stairs, following her husband.

"Might I ask your name?" I called from behind. "Maybe I could …"

"Of course," she said, glancing backward. "We're the Barneses. In flat three. Come and see us anytime you wish, dear."

"Oh, thank you so much."

I watched her descend the stairs as the train pulled into the station. Her husband Jack had bought their tickets, and they just managed to enter the train before its doors shut.

When I returned to the park my notebook was on the ground several metres from the picnic table, and the Chinese mother with her toddler was nowhere to be seen. A strong hot wind blew through the trees, sending a hand-size branch covered in eucalyptus leaves onto the top of the table. I picked up the branch and fanned my face with it, staring across the street into the dark pits that were balconies. Unable to concentrate, I picked up my notebook, gathered my papers and dictionaries and walked once again along the street, skirting the tracks to my flat in Gordon. I would visit Mr. and Mrs. Barnes the next day. I would bake a cake for them. I would find out who lived beside, above and below them. "When you bake *rabarbrakake* with rhubarb and dill," my mother had said to me when I was a little girl in Moji, "you know it's spring and that good things are about to come your way." I had always craved a piece of that cake when it had just come out of the oven. The smell was divine. I clearly recall begging my mother for just one slice. "This is not for you, Liv. It's for the people who are devoting themselves to your father's church work."

I baked that cake from a handwritten recipe my mother had left among her effects. Mother would not be proud of me, baking her beloved spring cake merely to ingratiate myself with an old couple in a block of flats, to use them to get to someone I was convinced I once knew. That little cake would be a means to an end. I was just like that little girl in the leek-green dress standing as high as she could to see over the heads of people. The only difference between me and her was that I was alone. I had no strong brothers to stand behind. I had no kindly aid workers to comfort and save me. I had to rely entirely on myself. If it meant getting to *that man*, I would do anything. I baked a ramekin of rhubarb cake just for myself and ate it after smothering it in cream. It was delicious. I was indulging myself for the first time in years. Why shouldn't I? Why shouldn't I indulge myself? I hadn't been able to do so as a child. I had not even done it in Australia, where the freedom of self-indulgence is seen as both a right and a duty. From now on, I promised myself, my personal satisfaction was something that I was going to pursue with a vengeance.

Martin came into bed every night seething with anger. He was the gentlest person I have ever known, and yet he couldn't control his desire to harm Donald Meissner.

"You must not attack him, darling," I said to Martin, pulling his hand towards my chest, flattening his palm over my breasts and gently stroking his fingers one by one. "It will destroy you sooner than it will destroy him."

"Why not? He is a beast. He has done the most horrific things and will continue to do so as long as this war lasts. Someone has to stop him."

"He may be acting like a beast but he is a human being. You cannot harm or, worse, kill someone. If you do, you become like him."

"He can. He can harm and kill at will. He eliminates lives without so much as blinking an eye."

"The war cannot go on much longer. We both have heard foreign broadcasts and seen secret cables, even ones from Berlin that reflect the real situation. Hitler cannot hold back Soviet troops past the summer."

"That's still half a year away, Liv. It's too long!"

"Shh, darling, don't let yourself get like this."

I kissed him on the lips and moved his hand down my stomach.

"I'm sorry, Liv. I'm just too upset right now."

"So Meissner is not just presenting us with a moral dilemma, he's ruining our sex life as well. He's like God and the Devil combined."

"He must be gotten rid of in some way."

Martin sat up in bed and lit a cigarette.

"You and I both know," I said, "that Germany and Japan are sure to lose the war. The Japanese are already trying to sue for peace in Moscow. When the Americans win, Donald Meissner will be headed straight for military prison. They won't let him out for years, if ever."

"No. They'll execute him for sure. Men like him have been executed by victors in the past for much much less."

"No, they shouldn't do that. If they kill him, they will be guilty of the same kind of murder that he is guilty of."

"Not the same kind. Liv, your innocence is so admirable. I love it, and I love you for it. But innocence is overshadowed during war by the worst crimes and sins. It is a luxury reserved for peacetime."

"Innocence has nothing to do with it, mine or anyone else's. There is only one kind of murder, whoever is holding the gun."

"Oh Liv, your thoughts are so beautiful. Did you inherit them from your parents?"

"Not at all. They loved God so much they were willing to believe that He had good reasons for doing away with His enemies."

"In normal times, yes. I would feel as you do," said Martin, stubbing out his cigarette, turning towards me and resting his head in his palm. "But at times like these, in a place like Tokyo in February 1945, charity and humankindness can lead to only one consequence—self-destruction. I will not stand by and watch a man like him destroy you and me just because we consider ourselves too good to take revenge on him. Why must good people always be sacrificed because they are too timid to counter evil? Now," he said, lifting his head and placing his palms over my breasts, "enough talk. There is no god or devil in this room. Kiss me again and make me feel good."

The carpetbombing of Japan had not yet begun and we still felt safe sleeping in a room in an old house near the centre of the city. The retribution we both feared most was not from the Americans but from Donald Meissner, the embassy's Gestapo liaison officer in charge of ties with the Japanese Military Police Corps, the Kempeitai. He was well aware that Martin and I despised him and his methods. But for the time being he had greater enemies than us in the German community. After all, he could keep an eye on us. But once the bombing of Tokyo began in March, even he began to question the certainty of victory. It was then that he turned his attention to us. He had to ensure that no one would be left to denounce and condemn him once Tokyo had fallen to the Americans and he would be at their mercy.

I stood at the front door of the block of flats on Marian St. and pressed the button beside the name "Barnes." There was no answer. I pressed it again, holding the rhubarb cake in a glass bowl covered with a cotton tea towel. After a moment I heard Mrs. Barnes's voice coming through the little speaker above the buttons.

"Yes, who's calling?"

"Oh, I'm so sorry to bother you, Mrs. Barnes. It's the lady from yesterday who accosted, well not exactly accosted, you and your husband outside yesterday. Oh, I'm repeating myself. I've, um, brought you ..."

"Oh yes. What was your name?"

"Liv. Liv Grimstad. It's spelled L-I-V but pronounced like 'leave.' I really shouldn't ..."

"Oh no, it's fine. I was just in the loo. Sorry to not answer immediately. Please do come up, dear."

A buzzer sounded, tripping the lock to the heavy front door. I entered the building, shutting the door behind me. The entryway was musty. The carpet, once no doubt luxurious, was worn down in places to its weave. The stairway was made of maple wood with rubber strips along the stair edges to prevent slipping. I climbed the stairs. There were two darkly stained oak doors on either side of the carpeted landing, each with a black metal number over a peephole: 3 … and 4. Could he be living across from Mr. and Mrs. Barnes? Would they meet occasionally, by chance, on the landing and exchange pleasantries? Could that nice elderly couple even conceive of the fact—no, not yet a fact—that they were living opposite the devil himself? Would anything he said or did betray him? No, he was too careful to allow something like that to happen. He would be too afraid that the past would catch up on him and reveal his real self to his "new" self. He would so cleverly disguise the rancid smell on him with sweet cologne. That is what was running through my mind as I knocked on the door with the number 3 nailed to it. The past will definitely catch up on you, Donald Meissner. You may have "moved on"—I laughed out loud when the words "moved on" rang loudly in my mind—but the past has moved along together with you, just a few steps behind you, right here just behind you, Herr Meissner, in the person of this innocent girl, now a woman, now only steps—no, a breath—away from you!

The door opened before I could knock, and Mrs. Barnes greeted me once again with a kindly smile.

"Oh, is that for me?" she said, pointing to the covered bowl. "I am so sorry, Mr. Barnes is out just now. He's gone into the city. But do come in, Liv, was it?"

"Oh, thank you. But it's not pronounced 'live.' My name is pronounced 'leave.' It's a Norwegian name."

"Oh, Norwegian," she said, clasping her hands together in front of her chest. "How very lovely. We have many new Australians in Sydney now but I've never met a Norwegian before. Jack, that's Mr. Barnes, loves Swedish people. He fought with them during the war. Or, no, I tell a lie, it wasn't Swedish people at all. I'll have to ask him. Well, please don't stand there. Do come in. Would you like a nice cuppa?"

"Oh, yes please. This is a rhubarb cake. My mother used to make it."

"Oh how very lovely. Thank you so much. Make yourself at home, please."

She shut the door behind me and went into the kitchen. The living room was gloomy, with thick floral-print curtains drawn over the windows and a standard lamp with a massive fringed shade in the corner spreading a creamy sheen over the furniture. I stood in the middle of the room. The oil paintings on the wall were landscapes of what looked like the English countryside. I sank down into a dark maroon Chesterfield sofa, almost losing my balance.

"Those're from Jack's grandparents who came out in the 1880s, I mean the paintings. The sofa's not that old," said Mrs. Barnes, coming into the room with a silver tray. "The sofa's wonderful to sit in, but once you're in it you can't get out. I've said to Jack, we'll both one day just sit ourselves in the sofa and never get up again."

She put the tray on a round table that was covered in a light-yellow lace cloth.

"This table cover was Jack's granny's. She made it herself. People had skills then. Milk or sugar?"

"No thank you. Just black, please."

"Well, you're not English, that's for sure. I took the liberty of putting some clotted cream beside the slices of cake."

"Oh yes, we eat it like that in Norway too, not that I've really spent much time in my country."

"No? That's interesting, to be from a country one doesn't know. I wouldn't know. I've never been out of Australia. Jack's the traveller in the family. But I have been overseas once, however."

"You have? I don't understand. If you've never left Australia...."

"Oh, Tasmania."

"I see," I chuckled.

"What's funny about that? Haven't you been over to Tassie?"

"Um, no. I haven't travelled much around Australia, actually. I spent my younger years in different places. I decided when I came to Australia to stay in one quiet place and just sit it out there."

"Here you are, dear," she said, passing me the cup and saucer. "Sure you don't want sugar? I've got lumps."

"Oh no, thank you."

"Sit it out? What do you mean?" she said after a moment's silence. "Are you not happy here?"

She eased herself down onto the sofa beside me.

"Oh, I didn't mean it in a negative sense. It's, you know, a language thing. English is not my native language. I do like it here but ..."

"No, you speak very well, although you do have an accent, you know."

"Yes, of course."

"It's, well, a kind of German accent. Not that I would know."

I took a sip of the tea, placing a dollop of cream on top of the slice of cake and cutting off a piece with the side of my fork.

"I hope you like the cake, Mrs. Barnes," I said.

"Oh, please do call me Gladys, or even Glad. That's what my friends call me. Oh, delicious," she said, swallowing a mouthful. "It's like, a little like that strudel thing, you know, the apple one. You must give me the recipe."

"Gladly. Um, Gladys?"

I put my fork down without having eaten the piece of cake on it.

"Yes. Would you like a top up?"

"No, thank you. The tea's fine. Um, I was wondering about

the other flats, if, um, someone might be moving or perhaps willing to sell. Do you know the other people here?"

"Oh yes, Jack and I know everyone, not that there are so many to know here. We have our strata meetings, you know, which we must have. Everyone comes, you know. We are a friendly bunch, all of us. We don't bicker like a lot of your flat dwellers."

"Is, well, is everyone here a family? That is, is there someone who is living alone, say, an elderly man, person, who might wish to give up a flat to someone like me?"

"Yes, there is one man who lives here alone."

"I see. Which flat number is he in?"

Just then the front door opened and Mr. Barnes walked in.

"Oh, what is it, dear? Did the RSL Club get-together end already?"

"No, I was just feeling a tad crook. I left not long after I got to the club."

"Oh my goodness. What is it?"

"Dunno. Oh hello. Sorry. It's awful barging in on guests like this. You're the nice lady from the park, aren't you?"

"Yes, dear, this is, oh, I'm afraid I've forgotten how to pronounce your name."

"Liv."

"I think I'd better have a Bex and a little lie down. I'm really feeling rather crook."

Having said that, he reeled about and fell forward, breaking his fall by grasping onto an arm of the sofa with both hands.

"Oh my goodness, Jack, are you all right?"

He stood up, but his knees were shaking.

"I'm afraid I'll have to be looking after Jack here. I'm so sorry. Do you mind? Please come again whenever you wish. And thank you so much for the cake. Can you let yourself out?"

"Um, yes, sure."

I stood up from the sofa. The front door had been left ajar. I walked out and was shutting it when I heard Mrs. Barnes's voice coming from the bedroom.

"Thank you! Please come again. I'll return your bowl and tea towel then."

I waited on the landing for some time, contemplating whether I should knock on the door opposite or, indeed, go to all the other flats to see where that man was living. But I came to the conclusion that such an action might ruin my chances of delving further into his life. The first real encounter had to appear to be a coincidence, even if it was a coincidence that I had calculated to occur.

Several weeks passed. No matter how many times I sat in the park, working on my translation, I did not catch him leaving the block of flats. A few other people left and entered—a tall young blond couple with a four- or five-year-old daughter, a dark-haired middle-age woman who looked Italian or Greek, and various deliverymen—but not *him*. The deadline for submitting the translation had passed and I had phoned the translation service company that had commissioned it asking for more time. They had extended the deadline by five days. I was finding it increasingly difficult to work. I would stare at the Chinese characters in the text and somehow be unable to decipher them. It was as if their lines and strokes were vibrating or swimming before my eyes. I constantly looked up to the six black pits of the balconies as if fully expecting a lone figure to appear out of one of them and stare back at me. The intervals of my looking up kept getting shorter and shorter. I could not bear leaving more than thirty seconds without checking ... then fifteen ... and ten. It then occurred to me that the two instances I had seen him on the train had occurred at the same time of day. He had taken the train from Roseville Station at around half past one. If I rode on that very train every day I would be sure to meet up with him again. "Oh hello," I would say. "This is a coincidence. We seem to be travelling at the same time in the same car. Do you remember me? I am the lady who picked up your stick. Do you live in Roseville? I couldn't help but notice that you get off the train at Killara. I live at the next stop, Gordon. Have you lived long around here? Are you from Sydney? Did you come to Australia from Europe? Germany, perhaps ... after the war? Did you come here to forget what happened to you in Europe, or to repress the memories of what you were, *who* you were?" My mind was racing ahead. My mind was getting away from me. I could not truly approach him in this way. I would have to find a cleverer means of getting to him.

I heard my phone ringing when I arrived at my front door. I reached into my handbag for the keys. They weren't in the inside pocket where I always placed them. I thrust my hand to the bottom of the bag. Still no keys. The phone continued to ring. I turned my bag upside down, spilling its contents on the welcome mat. I grabbed the front door key and tried to put it in the lock, but it wouldn't go in. The phone was still ringing. I turned the key right side up and slipped it into the lock. Leaving the front door open I rushed to the phone, but when I put the receiver to my ear all I heard was an uninterrupted buzz. I returned to the door and gathered up my things. Who would be calling me? With the exception of unsolicited calls from businesses and charities, I hadn't been phoned by anyone in months.

The phone rang again. I rushed to the receiver.

"Is that Grimstad-san?" a man said in Japanese.

"Yes."

"This is Takeshita from Northbridge Translation Services."

"Oh, Takeshita-san."

"Grimstad-san. I have been phoning you every day but no one has been at home."

"I am so sorry. I have had, um, some personal things to

attend to. But I am working on the Toyota translation. No, I mean the Hitachi translation. I know that the deadline has passed. And thank you for extending it for me."

"In Japanese there is really only one deadline. I did not extend it. Our policy is to tell our translators a false deadline earlier. We must protect our clients, Grimstad-san."

"Yes, of course."

"I regret to have to inform you that we have given your job on this to someone else."

"But I am almost finished with it. I was going to post it to you soon."

"I regret to say that it is too late. Such is the clause in our contract with you. Please read it. Please take a rest and do your personal things. We will be in touch with you in the future, I am sure. Do not call us. We will call you."

"I see."

"Thank you for your understanding, Grimstad-san. *Shitsurei shimasu* (Goodbye)."

Again I heard the uninterrupted buzz. I replaced the receiver. My notebook and dictionaries were sitting in a neat pile beside the phone.

"Oh well," I sighed to myself. That's all. Just "oh well." I had saved up enough money over the years of doing translation and interpreting jobs for Japanese executives visiting Australia. I didn't have to work for some time. I was free to pursue *that man*. I was going to stop at nothing. "You have all the time in the world." That's what I told myself as I lay down fully clothed on my bed and, moments later, was lost to sleep.

Martin had arrived at the embassy in 1943, two years after me. He had been transferred from Shanghai. We shared an office with a Japanese man named Inomata. The three of us spoke English together.

"I wish I spoke Japanese like you, Liv," said Martin several days after starting work at the embassy.

"But my German is terrible. And you speak Chinese so well," I said. "Not to mention English so fluently. Why is your English so good, Martin?"

"English is more important than Japanese," said Inomata-san. "After the war, whoever wins, Japan will have to become friendly again with the United States."

"What do you mean by 'whoever wins,' Mr. Inomata?"

Martin, furrowing his brow, had said this with an ironic scowl.

"Oh, I was speaking only for Japan," said Inomata-san. "It goes without saying that Germany will win the war. After all, it isn't called the Thousand-Year Reich for nothing, is it?"

That sort of conversation was typical for our room upstairs at the end of the corridor at the Embassy of Germany in Tokyo.

"We have a nice view of the Diet building from here, don't we," said Inomata-san, standing at the window looking out. "I was working here when it was completed seven years ago. The *rippofu* is right under our nose. Oh, Liv-san, how do you say *rippofu* in English?"

"Legislature."

"She's a genius, I tell you," said Inomata-san.

Martin smiled at me.

"No genius. I acquired both Japanese and English as a child living in Kyushu. I played with Japanese children and children of missionaries from Australia and Great Britain. You two are the geniuses. You had to learn your languages the hard way."

Martin was now standing beside Inomata-san at the window.

"What's that building there, the one with the fancy door there?"

"Ah," said Inomata-san. "That's the Rikugunsho. That I do know. It's the Army Ministry of Japan, commonly referred to by non-Japanese people as the Ministry of War. That door is the staff entrance. You can see plainly from here who comes and goes. Have you been to the room on the opposite end of the corridor here?"

"No."

"Well, it's locked, unless you have a key. Only a very few personnel have one. From the outside the Venetian blinds are always shut. But through an opening in the blinds in that room there is constant surveillance of the staff entrance of the Ministry of War building."

"You mean we Germans spy on our trusted allies?"

I did not know Martin well enough then to sense whether this was another expression of irony or simply a question made in all innocence.

"Spy? Never heard of such a thing," said Inomata-san. "Have you, Liv-san?"

"How should I know?" I said. "I just translate Japanese documents into English for the ambassador. I don't bother myself with the content, just the words."

I smiled at Martin. He walked across the room and placed his hand flat on my desk, staring at me in silence.

"Just about the time you joined us two years or so ago, Liv-san," said Inomata-san, "things were a bit different. Ambassador Ott was more—how do you say?—liberal than Ambassador Stahmer. Stahmer worked directly under Reich Minister for Foreign Affairs von Ribbentrop. Ott was—how do you say?—a softie?"

Both Martin and I chuckled.

"Yes, Inomata-san. Very good," I said.

"Yes, a very softie, can I say? Eugen Ott was a general, but of the old school. They transferred him out of here to Pekin, where he is now. He was the one who gave such free access in the embassy to Richard Sorge, who is now in a Japanese prison for spying for the Soviets."

"I met Sorge in Shanghai," said Martin.

"What was he like?" I asked.

"I never got to know him well. I was of the wrong sex. In addition, he could drink any man *unter den Tisch*, under the table. I collapse into a heap after two beers. I'm afraid I am not a very good German."

I woke up. The Sony digital clock given to me by a visiting Japanese executive said 4:45. It was still dark outside, and the magpies were filling the air with their flute-like calls. I went to the kitchen, filled my plastic electric kettle, switched it on and unfolded the train schedule for the North Shore Line that I had picked up at Gordon Station. It made no sense to go to Roseville Station before seven. It would be unlikely that he would arrive there that early. What was the purpose of his going there? I knew there was a Returned Servicemen's Club near the station, but that man, of all people, would hardly be visiting a club for Australian war veterans.

I arrived at Roseville Station shortly after seven thirty. I stepped out of the train as a line of businessmen carrying attaché cases brushed past me, rushing to get a seat in the crowded car. Dozens of schoolgirls dressed in the uniforms of the posh private schools to the north were waiting for the train to come from the city. I sat on a platform bench near the front of the train. I didn't want him to catch sight of me as the train pulled into the station. Unless he was sitting in the front car, which was unlikely because it was not the closest car to the station stairs, he would not see me. A man in his condition, walking as he did with a stick, would choose the car closest to the stairs.

Three hours passed and he had not appeared.

"Excuse me. Are you all right?"

The stationmaster, a man who looked no older than a

teenager, was standing in front of me. The sun shone behind his head and I had to squint to see his face properly.

"Oh, sorry, I can see that I'm standing in the sun," he said, stepping to one side. "Are you all right? I noticed that you've been here a long time."

"I'm waiting for someone. Thank you."

"Ah, I see. No worries," he said, pursing his lips into a grin and nodding his head. "Well, I do hope he'll show. Uh, would you like to use the phone in the office? The red phone on the platform sort of works but on and off, know what I mean? Telecom has taken the phones over but they haven't got around to maintaining the ones in the stations yet."

"No, thank you. I will just wait a little longer. You're very kind."

He dipped his cap and walked away, stopping to pick up a small wad of chewing gum with his bare hands. The platforms were quiet now, with only a few people, mostly old men and middle-aged women, getting on and off the trains. I decided to wait only fifteen minutes longer, until eleven. Then I would go home. No, I wouldn't go home. I would take the train to the city and walk around the Opera House. In the two years since its opening I had only seen it from the window as the train crossed the bridge. I would wait for the train that arrived at five minutes to eleven and take it to the city.

I saw the train approaching and stood up. But what if he was on that train? I should stay where I was by the front car and wait. I had to wait as long as it took. I would wait for him forever.

I was standing at the window of our room in the embassy. Martin was beside me. Inomata-san had taken ill and was to stay away for the week.

"Look," said Martin. "It's Donald Meissner. He's waiting

at the staff entrance of the Ministry of War. Look how erect he stands. I swear, that man was born standing to attention. When he came out of his mother's womb, the midwife didn't say 'It's a boy' but 'It's a soldier.' When he waved his little hand for the first time, it was in the form of a salute."

"What's so strange about him being there and looking like that? The Japanese adore formality. It's what they admire most in the Germans. They don't care what you do so long as you do it with discipline and decorum."

"Yes, some Germans are like that. And with everybody else? What do they do then?"

"What do you mean? I don't understand."

"Never mind. Liv?"

"What?"

"The Japanese. With everybody else, the Japanese look down on them. It makes it easier for them to treat them like dirt. They can only look up or down, never to someone on their own level."

"I don't agree, Martin. Japanese people before the war were kind and considerate. Their language is formal, but they treat people equally."

"Maybe. You know much better than I. Believe me, I never used to be so cynical. I trusted everyone. Maybe that was my problem."

"You're just upset by what that one man is doing."

"No, I'm upset by what 80 million Germans are doing. Now, let's put this argument aside," he said, sitting on the window sill. "I've been here six weeks and this is the first time you and I have been alone together."

"We work together," I said, feeling somewhat uncomfortable. "I mean …"

"Yes, work. And once this war is over, 'whoever wins,' to quote Inomata-san, where will you go?"

"I don't know. I'll probably stay here. I've lived most of my life in Japan."

"But you're not Japanese."

"No, I'm not. But this has been my home."

"I understand," he said, taking a cigarette from his shirt pocket and lighting it with a large silver lighter. "You don't smoke, right?"

"No. Thank you."

He inhaled deeply and blew the smoke into the velvet curtains.

"I might go back to China, who knows?"

"Did you feel at home there?"

"Oh yes. I love the people."

"What about the people in your own country."

"Germany? Love? Who could love such a people now? They have all gone insane."

"But you are working in the embassy. Is this the embassy of the insane then?"

"When I joined the foreign service, many of us were anti-Nazi. The hatred for Hitler and his thugs was strong. We thought we could still do something once on the inside. But we were deluded, all of us. Some of my friends were arrested and executed. Others, like me, left Germany just to get away. We just did not want to be near those criminals. I was so naïve, Liv. I thought the war would be over by the end of 1940 or 1941 at the latest. So naïve. So stupid."

He stubbed the cigarette out in the ashtray on the window sill.

"Do you mind me talking like this? Don't worry. No one else knows how I feel. But you are not German, so I thought you would understand."

"Of course I do not agree with what Germany and Japan are doing. There is so much cruelty."

"Someday Germans will come to their senses. Think of the philosophers we have produced, the composers, the poets, the artists! It is they who represent us, not the henchmen of fascism. When this is all over—and it will be all over—we must never again allow those people to speak for us and act in our name. That was the crime of all Germans—apathy, and tolerance of an evil that we deluded ourselves into thinking would pass us by, like a parade of depraved clowns, and disappear over the horizon forever."

"Japan turns out to be my country ... by default."

"Go to China and see what your wonderful Japanese are doing there."

"Who said they were wonderful?"

"Murdering children with bayonets by throwing them up in the air and stabbing them. Raping women and little girls." He picked up the stub and rolled it in his fingers, letting unburnt tobacco leaves fall into the ashtray. "Well, who am I to talk? We slaughter people by the tens of thousands. Have you heard about the concentration camps?"

"Which concentration camps? I know the British had them in places."

"No. Our own German ones. Oh, the British camps were not a patch on ours. We Germans are known for our scientific skills."

I stared at Martin. He had tears in his eyes.

The train came to a stop and a few passengers began to alight. I was stepping into the front car when I saw him, first his stick, then his right leg, then the body and head. He had come! I quickly stepped backward onto the platform again, stumbling and swinging my arms to steady myself. Luckily he did not see this, though he was in the second car and only some ten metres away from me. I swiveled about, so that if he did look at me he would see only the back of my head. I was standing below the stairs and could glimpse his stick being placed on one stair after another.

He waited at the traffic light to cross the Pacific Highway, and I stood in the shadow of a nearby building with my back against its wall. The light changed and he crossed. I followed. He walked with an even and slow pace past the RSL Club and the park beside it, turning the corner. I waited until he disappeared to follow him down the hill on a street called Maclaurin Parade. Had he turned around he would have seen me. He would surely have recognized me from our previous encounters, however fleeting, on the train. But he wouldn't turn around, would he. No, he would not. I knew that. That man had lived for thirty years in safety. No one would bother to follow him now. No one would know what kind of a man he had been before. No one would wish to confront him now and say to him, "This is you. Your past is your present. You cannot walk away. Not from me!"

It took him nearly ten minutes to walk down the hill, stopping under crepe myrtle trees on the nature strip. When he stopped I retreated into a driveway, slouching behind a car, a Toyota Hilux ute with PYMBLE PLUMBERS painted across its panels. He resumed his walk down the hill, crossing the street and turning into a narrow street, virtually an alleyway, called Nola Road.

I crossed the street opposite the driveway and went to the corner of Nola Road. There was no sign of him. Nola Road was a cul-de-sac with only a few large houses set far from the street, with a creek running beside it and grounds overgrown in eucalyptus, casuarina, king ferns, bottle brush and other native trees. He must have gone into one of those houses. I would have to carefully engineer the first real meeting with him. But I couldn't very well front up to those houses and knock on their doors.

I had also been with him once on the train going the other way in the early afternoon. I could have lunch and a cup of tea at a café by the cinema on the Pacific Highway. If I sat in the window I would see him walking on his way back to the station. Should I follow him back onto the train? "Oh, haven't we met before on this train?" "Yes, I believe so. You were the kind lady who retrieved my stick from the floor. I never forget a face." Don't you? Good. Then you will remember mine. You *will*!

I decided, however, to wait on the corner of Maclaurin Parade and Nola Road until he started his walk back up the hill to the station. I could see part of the houses through the trees and shrubs. I might be able to determine which one he emerged from if I didn't take my eyes off those houses. My eyes flitted from one to the other. I would not miss him at any cost. I was famished and my mouth was dry, but I would forego eating and drinking if it meant that I would find out where he was going on these trips to Roseville.

It was shortly after one that I saw him ambling up Nola Road towards the corner. I had failed to see which house he had left. But it wouldn't be hard to go to them all once he was gone. I would discover his every move, follow his every step.

So as not to be seen by him I entered the front garden of the house on the corner and crouched behind a bush, nearly stomping on a small anthill between the bush and the outside wall of the house. Large ants were crawling all around and on top of the hill, and some of them climbed onto my feet. I was wearing sandals with no stockings, but I ignored the ants as I observed him crossing the street and making his way up the slope of the street. It wasn't until he turned the corner on the Pacific Highway that I stood, frantically brushing large ants off my shins, calves and thighs.

I went first to the end of the cul-de-sac where a stately white home stood. It was clearly Victorian, with black iron railings on its upstairs terrace. A sign running across the terrace read: NOLA ROAD NURSING HOME. This seemed to be the most logical place for him to have gone. At least it was a form of public building, much easier to enquire at than a private home.

I stood at the front door rehearsing what I would say. I had done that since the time I was a little girl. Whatever attitude the other person, particularly adults, would confront me with, I felt on safe ground if I knew what I was going to say beforehand. I rang the doorbell. A young Asian woman in a nurse's uniform opened the door. A badge above the nurse's watch pinned to her blouse read: VICTORIA.

"May I help you?"

"Oh yes. Excuse me. This is my first time here. My mother is elderly and not as strong as she used to be. I came because I wished to enquire about the possibility of her coming to live here. I have heard so many good things about your home."

I had known since childhood that adding words of praise, whether true or not, was always the best way to slip yourself into someone's good books.

"Thank you. Our business manager, who handles that sort of thing, is off today. But she will be back tomorrow at eight-thirty a.m. Could you possibly come back then? Do you live in the vicinity?"

"Oh yes. That's no problem."

"Fine then. May I ask your name?"

"But then there is another thing."

"Another thing?"

"Yes. That man who was just here."

"Yes."

"I mean, as he walked up the street I noticed from a distance that he had dropped something. By the time I got to the place he had turned onto the highway. I noticed that he had come from here so I picked it up and brought it. It's a key. I hope it's not one he needs. If it is I guess he'll come back or something."

I took out the spare house key that I carried in the zippered pocket of my handbag.

"How very kind of you. There aren't many kind people like you these days. Everyone thinks only of himself. Thank you. I'll leave it with his wife. He comes here just about every single day to visit her. He is such a nice man, the nicest and most generous person amongst all our visitors."

I was so taken aback by her praise of him that I felt myself unable to speak. My mouth had suddenly dried out, and I rubbed my tongue against my palate over and over again to produce saliva.

Nurse Victoria's eyes opened wide, as if she was struck with worry about me.

"Shall I give Margaret the key then?" she said.

"Oh yes, thank you. Thank you."

"Would you like to come in for a moment? I think it would be okay if you had a look around, even if Mrs. Archibold isn't here. She's the business manager. Would you like a cup of tea? You look, uh, thirsty."

Being a nurse she could obviously tell that I was not myself.

"Oh yes, that would be lovely. Thank you so much."

She led me into the main room, where some residents were seated in old armchairs and others at a long wide oak table. The thick curtains were drawn over the windows. Light was provided by a chandelier hanging over the centre of the room and a number of table lamps with alabaster shades. Most of the residents were asleep.

"There's Margaret, over there," said Nurse Victoria, pointing to an old woman sitting in a dark-brown leather armchair beside a window. She was staring straight ahead as if into the distance.

We walked over to her.

"Margaret, this is a friend of your husband's," said Nurse Victoria, smiling at me.

"How do you do?" said Margaret, gazing at me for a moment, then looking askance.

"Very nice to meet you, Margaret," I said.

"She has your husband's key. So let's make sure he gets it tomorrow. I'll just put it in your little bag."

I handed the nurse the key and she placed it carefully in a small cloth bag, zipping it up.

"She won't remember it, but I'll make sure the other nurse who comes in tomorrow knows about it. I'm off tomorrow for a time."

"Holiday?"

"Pardon?"

"Are you going on holiday?"

"Uh, yes and no. I'm going to Hong Kong where my own mother lives. She needs looking after now apparently."

The "apparently," spoken emphatically, indicated to me not only that she had not seen her mother in a long time, but that she was none too pleased at having to go to her.

"Look, it's all right, just forget the key," I said. "Please don't mention it. I'm sure her husband will have a look in her bag and find it. He must have a spare."

"Well, all right, if that's what you want. At any rate, she doesn't know him."

"What do you mean?"

"She doesn't recognize anyone. She's seventy-two and apparently has been pretty much this way for three or four years. I came here about eighteen months ago and she was already here. Even though Mr. Miles visits her every day, and even washes her and changes her nappy, not once has she acknowledged that she knows he is her husband. It's so sad to see an angel of a man having to go through that. They must have been very fond in their younger years."

That man … an angel? I must have winced, because Nurse Victoria was ogling me again as if I was one of her patients.

"Look, let me get you that cup of tea."

She left the room through large French doors. One of the

residents, a scrawny man who might have been ninety, was standing in the very middle of the room, taking off one item of clothing after another. He sat down and began removing his trousers. Some of the other residents—the ones who were awake enough to notice—stared at him with blank expressions.

By the time Nurse Victoria returned with a mug of tea in her hands the man was entirely naked, waving his hands wildly in the air and doing some sort of dance under the chandelier.

"Oh dear," she said, handing me the cup. "Be careful, it's hot. Oh dear. Mr. Somerset, please, we must not do that here."

She rushed to him, picked up his shirt and wrapped it around his waist, tying the sleeves together at the back.

"Now, now, we are naughty, aren't we."

She retrieved all of his clothing from the floor and led him out another door, turning towards me just before she reached it and smiling at me.

"Thank you so much," I said to her. "Thank you!"

MILES ... with a wife named Margaret. That was a beginning, and the first piece of information that led me to my initial "coincidental" encounter with that man. I wonder if he had kept his first name—Donald.

That night I barely slept a wink. All I had for dinner was a cup of instant coffee and an apple. So his name was Miles, which meant that he did live in the flat opposite Mr. and Mr. Barnes, flat number 4. I had been standing on the landing by his very door. I could have knocked. He was certain to be in at that time of day. "Yes, madam, what can I do for you?" "Do for me? Look at me, you filthy beast! Look at my face. Do you recognize me? It has only been thirty years. People do not change that much, not physically." "I'm sorry, madam, but I do not know you. Now, please leave. I was napping." "Napping? It is an amazement that you have been able to sleep at all these thirty years. Perhaps you have been up, calculating your next atrocity ... or have you been plagued by pangs of conscience?

No. No. A man must possess a conscience in the first place in order for it to haunt him." The door slams in my face. The sound is that of a fireball exploding in a corridor. Burning slivers shoot into the air, striking the walls and ceiling. There is a little girl in a light-green dress. The little girl is standing in that corridor. The papers in the box are on fire. Sparks crackle and jump. They jump onto her thin little dress. "MINAKO!" I scream out her name. "LIV!" She screams out mine. I turn to her. She is lying on her back on the floor. I cover her with my whole body. My body snuffs out the flames that were about to engulf her.

I was not dreaming. This was racing through my awake mind. I covered my ears with my palms. Minako's scream was reaching me thirty years after it had left her lips.

I needed to be perfectly sane and logical if I was going to do this right. I would go to the Nola Road Nursing Home in the morning and present myself as a volunteer. Nurse Victoria wouldn't be there so I need not repeat the story about my mother needing care. The home looked understaffed. Fortunately I had received a letter of recommendation from Dr. Alexander at the Scottish Hospital in Paddington where I had helped out on weekends for a year before volunteering for work at the refugee centre in Cabramatta. "Miss Grimstad is a model of dedication. She has shown admirable ability in looking after our patients, particularly our elderly and feeble ones. She is the most selfless person I have known."

I have made myself so self-effacing that I have been left with no face at all. This has been by choice. Perhaps "Mr. Miles" will not be able to recognize me at all. "I am sorry, madam, but you have no face. Please come back when you get your face back and then I may recognize you." That's droll, isn't it … a woman without a face but one who is spending her days in the service of others, always others, never herself. Nothing for the self. Why would she want to do something solely for herself?

She looks in the mirror. "Sorry, lady, but I don't recognize you. Your mouth is moving with mine but it is not my mouth. Your eyes are looking at me but they are not my eyes. Come back tomorrow morning and we'll have another look." How amusing this is! All right, Liv, pull yourself together. Walk over to the sink in the bathroom. Wash your face first. You want to make a good impression, don't you? Now … look! Yes, it is me. I am Liv. I recognize myself. I have come back to myself after thirty years and now I will make certain that I force *that man* to recognize himself in his mirror. I will clutch him and not let go of him until he does so.

I wore my most prim gear, a red and black cotton dress, dry cleaned and starched, that I had worn at the Scottish Hospital, the one that had all the old ladies sitting up in bed and saying, "My, don't you look a picture, dear!" I put on stockings, polished a pair of black pumps and set out for Gordon Station. It was half past seven, and the platform for the train going into the city was crowded with businessmen, each of them, it seemed, carrying a folded copy of The National Times under his arm.

I arrived at the nursing home just after eight-thirty. The front door was unlocked. I let myself in, went directly to the business office and knocked on the door.

"Come in," came a woman's voice.

I entered and shut the door behind me.

"May I help you?"

The woman, immaculately groomed with soft grey hair pinned back in a bun, looked up from her desk. A nameplate on her desk read—Mrs. Rose Archibold.

"Oh, good morning, Mrs. Archibold. Please forgive me for coming so early this morning unannounced. I was here yesterday to see you but …"

"Yes, I was off yesterday."

"Um, that's what I was told."

She put down a hand-held calculator, clasped her hands together on the desk and said, "What can I do for you?"

"Um, my name is Liv Grimstad and, well, I have done quite a bit of volunteer work, most recently at a refugee centre in Cabramatta. But as the centre is winding up its work and seeing that I live not far from here, in Gordon, actually, I was wondering, um, if you might not need a hand here. I think I am very good with old people. Here. I have a reference from the Scottish Hospital where …"

"The one in Paddington?"

"Yes. You know it?"

"Of course I do. My father worked there with Dr. MacCormick back in the twenties. It was such a shame."

"A shame?"

"Yes. Dr. MacCormick's son perished in World War I like so many other young Australians who had gone over. But it was that loss that inspired him to donate the hospital to the church, the Presbyterians, if I recall what my father told me, for them to run it. What a wonderful gesture that was! Sometimes it takes a great tragedy to bring out the good in people."

"Yes, I understand."

She took the letter from my outstretched hand.

"I see. This letter speaks very highly of you … Miss Grimstad?"

"Oh, please call me Liv."

"Liv. Yes, very highly. As a matter of fact, we are in a bit of a pickle right now. Let's see, what's today? Friday. We have many visitors on the weekend, and we have to make our residents as presentable as possible for them. Would you like to start tomorrow, Saturday?"

"Oh yes, thank you so much. I really only feel myself when I'm able to do things for other people."

"What a wonderful thing to say!"

She stood up and offered her hand. I shook it.

"Do you mind if I keep this letter for reference?"

"Oh no. Please do. That's why I brought it. Actually, I have been a bit naughty and xeroxed a few copies, you know, just in case."

"I wouldn't call that naughty. I'd call it judicious. You seem to be a very down-to-earth woman. I think you are just the kind of woman our residents need. Most of them do not know who they are. But that doesn't mean that they do not enjoy life. I'll confide something in you," she said, moving around the desk. "I'd reckon that some of them are happier in this life than they were in their earlier lives."

Before leaving I made a round of the sofas and chairs in the main room, greeting all of the residents with a smile and a few words. I glanced back at the office door. Mrs. Archibold was standing in it, watching me with obvious approval. After she turned back into her office and shut the door I went up to Margaret Miles. She was asleep with her chin against her chest. A thin stream of drool was running from the corner of her mouth onto her grey dress. I took a tissue from a box on the side table and gently wiped her mouth. I dropped the tissue into a small wooden bin beside her armchair. Then I carefully unzipped her little cloth bag and lifted my house key from it. I looked around the room. The old man who had stripped under the chandelier was standing with his back against the wall staring at me. He flashed me a big smile. I bowed my head, a custom that had stayed with me since my years living in Japan, and smiled back at him.

It was eight-thirty when I walked out of the home. The sun was shining through the branches of the tall paper-bark eucalyptus on the front lawn where a pair of rosellas were foraging for food, picking up what looked like seeds and putting them in their mouth with their claws. Should I wait for him? I would have to crouch behind bushes for what might be hours. No. I wanted my red and black dress to look as good as new the next day. I wanted to present myself in the best possible light tomorrow. Tomorrow I would have a conversation with him for the first time … in thirty years.

I walked briskly up the hill, jumping onto the train just before the doors shut, went home, carefully hung up my dress and fell onto my bed in my underclothes. In a matter of seconds I was dead to the world.

Martin and I were living together by the end of 1943. He was renting two rooms in a *geshuku*, a lodging house, at Ichiban-cho, not far from the embassy, though the proprietor, Mrs. Yoshida, was none too happy about a man and woman living in sin in her lodging house.

"She puts up with it," said Martin, "because it corresponds with her preconception of what us Westerners are like. We're all decadent and immoral."

"Even Germans? I thought that decadence and immorality were banned in Germany."

"Oh Liv, I do adore your sense of humour."

"Thank you, but it is well known that Norwegians do not have a sense of humour. Among the Scandinavians, it's only the Danes who know a good laugh when they hear one. We Norwegians are all dour and glum. The Swedes are worse, but they lack the self-knowledge to admit it."

"You dour and glum? You are the happiest-go-luckiest woman I know."

He kissed me on the tip of my nose and cupped his hands over my breasts.

"Oh no. Don't say that. My poor parents will be turning over in their graves. They were as far a cry from happy-go-lucky as you can get. No drinking. No frivolous entertainment, which included films, dancing, you know. You never know when the Saviour is going to return to Earth. If he finds you having fun and forgetting yourself even for a minute, you'll be judged harshly and you won't make it to the promised land."

"But they must have had sex."

"Who, my parents?"

"Yes."

"Once, yes."

"I'm glad they did. They gave birth to you, my saviour."

He rolled on top of me. He was so thin that I could feel his pelvic bones against mine. I found myself taking a deep short breath when his penis went into me.

"I love your breath on my face," he said, "when we make love. I love you, Liv. I love you with all my heart. When all this is over we will go to Norway. I don't want ever to return to Germany. We'll live out our lives there, on the shore of a fjord surrounded by tall cliffs, with our children, at least four of them. Liv, Liv, stop crying. Stop."

He rolled over onto his back.

"No, darling, please come into me again. I want you."

"I'll wait until you stop crying."

"I can't help it. It's not you. I love you so much, Martin. I love you. *Jeg elsker deg.* That's in Norwegian. I've never said it to anyone in any language. When you hold me in your arms I feel like we can never never be separated from each other, and it makes me feel too as if I can get through all this, through this horrible war. I don't want to live by a fjord. I picture us sitting on a bench in a park on a sunny day somewhere—I don't care where. We're holding hands, darling, and watching our little children do handstands and running over the grass in bright sunlight. That vision is the only thing that gives me something resembling hope."

"We will be happy. You deserve to be happy. You are such a kind and considerate person. I want you to start having a life of your own. You've had a childhood trying to make your parents believe that you love God. Now you are working for the Devil. We Germans are the world's devils. No, worse than devils. We are evil personified right here on Earth. It is hard to even imagine how a devil can be more vicious and brutal and exacting in it all. But we were once not like that. I swear, we will extricate ourselves from this hell one day and become the people we once were. Just a little longer, Liv. Just a little …"

I lifted myself up and lay on top of him.

"Oh Martin, I cannot imagine life without you now. Please please do not let anything happen to you."

"I won't, Liv. I promise. No one will come between us."

I woke up at seven p.m., baked two meat pies that I had kept in the freezer, watched a Don Lane Show Special and fell asleep again, not waking until five in the morning. I showered and put on the red and black dress. I pinned a *solje* silver brooch, a memento handed down to my mother from my grandmother, onto the dress. Its little hanging spoons seemed to be an appropriate symbol of what I was to do in my new volunteer work. "Ah, Liv," I said to myself in the mirror, "you haven't lost your dry sense of humour after all. I will spoonfeed the man's wife. Spoons will be the weapon to get to him. Everything will come back to you, Liv. Everything."

I arrived at the nursing home at eight and immediately began duties by carrying the breakfast dishes to the kitchen. A girl whose badge identified her as Magda was washing them.

"Just put them here, thank you. You new?"

"Yes. Liv is my name. Nice to meet you."

"Good to meet you. I am Magda. I work here six days a week."

"Oh, I'm just a volunteer. But I think I will be coming often."

"Working as a volunteer? Are you with a church or something?" she said, tossing a damp tea towel over her shoulder.

"Church? No. Just, um, helping out."

"Your mother here, or aunt or something?"

"No. Just, um …"

I was unable to come up with a reason for my being there that would satisfy her.

"Some people are just nice, I guess. Or rich enough to be able to afford to be nice."

She whisked the tea towel off her shoulder and started wiping bowls and cups.

"I think this is the last of the dishes," I said.

She nodded without saying anything.

When I returned to the main room all of the residents were seated in a circle. In the centre of the circle a young man with long hair, a beard and a bizarre array of large colourful beads around his neck was playing the guitar. He started to sing a song that I was unfamiliar with, beginning with the words "If You Knew Susie."

A male nurse whose badge read "Bill" was beside me, clapping his hands to the music, trying to get the residents to do the same. He knelt at the feet of an old balding woman in a wheelchair.

"Do you know my name?" he asked.

"No, I don't," said the woman, opening her mouth wide and resting her hand on his shoulder.

"I'm Bill," he said, twisting his badge up so that she could read it.

"Oh, hello Bill. Nice to meet you."

"Well, nice to meet you too," he said, standing and turning to me, adding, "they all think they are hearing my name for the first time, though I introduce myself to all of them every day. Hi, I'm Bill."

He was in his late twenties or early thirties, muscular, stocky and freckled all over his cheeks and nose.

"I'm Liv. That's spelled L-I-V. I'm starting today, just as a volunteer."

"That's wonderful. We need people like you. The residents respond immediately to our volunteers. They think they're their daughters or granddaughters. Don't disabuse them, please. Let them think it, even for a few short moments."

"Of course I will. I've worked with people like this before."

Margaret Miles was sitting in the circle, clapping her hands to the rhythm of the song that was just ending with the words "Oh what a gal!" The guitarist stood up and bowed. All of the residents seemed to come to life, giving him a round of applause.

I walked under the chandelier to her.

"Hello, Margaret. How are you today?"

"Fine thank you," she said in a clear voice with a distinct German accent. "How are you?"

"I'm very fine. Would you like to return to your armchair now?"

"Oh yes, thank you."

I helped her up and walked arm-in-arm with her to her chair beside the window.

"This is where I sit," she said.

"Yes, I know."

"You know? Have you been here before?"

"Yes, as a matter of fact, I have."

"Are you Karen?"

"No. I'm Liv."

"That's a beautiful name."

"Thank you. Who's Karen?"

"Why, that's my granddaughter. She comes here every Saturday. They tell me that all the time. Is today Saturday?"

"Yes, it is."

"Oh, please tell me before she comes. I want to look nice for her. She is my sweet mouse."

I snapped my head away from her and put my hand up to

my eye. I must not let the tears flow at the mere sound of a word or two. “My sweet mouse,” said Martin. “That’s what I’m going to call you from now on, *meine suesse maus.*”

“Are you okay?” asked Bill, touching my arm.

“Sure. Sometimes, you know, it’s just sad to see these old people without their memories.”

“You’ll be fine,” he said. “Oh no, he’s coming back.”

The guitarist, who had gone out for a smoke, was sitting back in his chair. He rested the guitar on his knee and said, “Now for one that’ll bring back memories for sure. ‘You Must Have Been a Beautiful Baby.’”

He began to sing, and gradually the residents started clapping their hands. I turned to Margaret. She was fast asleep in her armchair, a narrow shaft of bright yellow light from the edge of the curtain crossing her face.

It was a few minutes after ten when a beautiful young woman with a ponytail, dressed in a pink cotton skivvy and a plaid skirt, came into the home carrying a small bouquet of daisies. I was reading to one of the residents when I happened to look over the book and notice her walk to the window and stand in front of Margaret Miles. I shut the book—the old woman I was reading to was asleep anyway—and stood up.

“That’s Mrs. Miles’s granddaughter,” said Mrs. Archibold. “She comes here on Saturdays, sometimes with her mother.”

“I see.”

“Come over. I’ll introduce you.”

We approached them just as the young woman was handing her grandmother the bouquet.

“What am I supposed to do with this?” said Margaret.

“Here, I’ll take them,” said Mrs. Archibold.

“Who are these people?” asked Margaret with a puzzled look on her face.

“This is Liv. She’s working here now as a volunteer. And this is your granddaughter.”

"My granddaughter?"

"Yes. Karen, your granddaughter."

"Hello grandma."

"She doesn't look like my granddaughter. *She* looks like my granddaughter," she said, pointing to me.

"That's because you saw her at breakfast this morning."

"I'm your granddaughter, grandma. Marlis's daughter. Marlis is your daughter. She couldn't come today." She turned to Mrs. Archibold. "Mother's not well."

"I'm sorry to hear that."

"Oh I don't know," said Margaret, shaking her head and straightening the edges of the knitted travel rug draped over her lap.

"I'll stay with her for a while," said Karen.

Mrs. Archibold turned about and returned to her office.

"Did you just start here? I haven't seen you before."

"Yes. I'm new. It's kind of you to visit her."

"She's my grandma. Of course I would visit her. I remember her when she was herself. She was the life of the party, always giggling. It's hard to take, especially for Grandpa Dan."

"Don?"

"No, Dan. Daniel. My grandpa. He comes here just about every day. But mum's in hospital, St. Vincent's, and he's ..."

"Is she okay?"

"Yeah, she's all right. She's just had an operation and they just want to keep her in for a week or so. So he's gone over to see her today and won't be coming. It's not so easy for me to get up here. I live in Glebe. I wanted to get away from all the trees and birds and everything here on the North Shore where mum and my grandparents were living so I moved to the gritty city. Everybody's so white up here. Glebe's different. Really, uh, cosmopolitan. Mum approved. She's a city girl, my mum. Spent her childhood in Switzerland but then sort of grew up in L.A. Wish I could've grown up in L.A. This city is so daggy."

"So … when did your grandparents migrate to Australia?"

"Before I was born. I've lived my whole life in Sydney. Boring. Really boring, you know? But you're a new Australian, I can tell. Are you Swiss too?"

"Are your parents Swiss?"

"Yep. Zurich. That's where mum was born. I've seen her passport. In December 1930. But all this is probably boring you to tears."

"No. I find it fascinating. Really."

"Grandma, would you like something to drink?"

"Drink? Yes. Scotch and soda."

The old woman cackled, knowing full well that the only alcohol kept on the premises was rubbing alcohol.

"Would you like a cup of tea?" I asked.

"Could it be coffee?"

"Yes, sure. Is instant all right."

"Uh-huh."

She followed me into the kitchen. I filled up the aluminium kettle, set it on the cooker and turned on the gas, lighting the fire with a Redhead match.

"Are you a student?" I asked.

"Can you tell?"

"Well, not really. Well, actually … yes."

We both laughed.

"This is my last year at uni, though. I'm not doing honours. Next month's my last month trying to please my lecturers. Education by regurgitation, that's what I call it. I'm going to spend a year in Europe. Maybe even stay on forever. Who knows? That's where the real culture is."

"Going back to your roots?"

"Roots? Not that. I don't speak German, except for a few baby words. Dad was of Germanic descent too, but his people came out to South Australia in the 1830s. They planted some of the first grape vines for wine. He and mum met here in Sydney not long after my grandparents arrived from the U.S. No, I'm going to Italy. I've been studying Italian, not that I can speak it or anything. I want to go to Florence and Parma and Sienna and places, see the art, you know, and, more than anything really, just get away from this boring daggy philistine country. There's nothing in Australia, just a lot of people who came here because they wanted to get as far away from everywhere else as possible. Australia is as far away from everywhere as possible. It's not on the way to anywhere, except New Zealand and the South Pole."

The kettle was whistling. I turned off the gas, poured boiling water into a cup for her and mixed in a heaping teaspoon of Nescafe Espresso.

"Oh, I haven't seen this instant espresso before. That's ace."

She took a sip of her coffee as I dropped an Earl Grey teabag into a mug and filled it with water. We walked back into the main room together, holding our cups in front of us.

"Have you been to Italy?" she asked.

"Yes, sure. It's an amazing place."

I was lying. I had never been south of Germany in Europe. But I was determined to make friends with Karen and would say anything that helped me achieve my goal.

"Far out. One of my friends, Stan, he's been to Italy. Could you, I mean, could we meet and you could, I mean, tell me about it? I really don't know what to expect. I'm just going to go and see if I can get some kind of job or something and just, you know, live. That's what I want to do for once. Just live for myself. Look, I'll give you my number."

She ripped a piece of paper from a small notebook and wrote her name and phone number on it with a pencil that was lying on the oak table.

"I'd better have a few words with grandma. You never know. Something may just jog her memory. I won't stop trying. She was such a funny lady."

Karen sat down on the arm of her grandmother's chair and stroked her thin white hair. Her grandmother leaned her head against Karen's thigh and seemed to be smiling.

I left the nursing home in the late afternoon. I wouldn't need to hide behind bushes or put up with my legs crawling with ants. I wouldn't have to hide at all. I would get to Daniel Miles through his granddaughter. Daniel Miles—DM—the very same initials. I'll be seeing you, Donald Meissner. I loved saying that phrase to myself. "I'll be seeing you" ... and I even hummed the song and whispered the words to myself as I strolled up the hill in the direction of Roseville Station—"I'll be seeing you ... in *all* the old familiar places ...."

I unfolded the piece of paper Karen had given me. Above her phone number was her name: Karen Ditzen. I felt that I didn't need to hurry anymore now that I knew I would reach her grandfather. I now had all the time in the world.

Donald Meissner entered our room without knocking. He paced around it, weaving between our desks, as he unbuttoned his stiff collar with its oak-leaf patches indicating that he was a high-ranking officer in the SS.

"Good morning, Martin. Liv. Herr Inomata. It is so very nice to see you three, as always. The Three Musketeers of the German embassy. Ha ha."

"*Ohayo gozaimasu* (Good morning)," said Inomata-san. He made it a point to speak only Japanese with Donald Meissner.

"Ah, Herr Inomata, I know that you speak fluent German. No doubt better than I do. But you insist on speaking Japanese with me. You know my proficiency in Japanese is nothing to boast about."

"*Ie ie, ojozu desu yo* (No no, you're very good at it)," he said. Then he added Meissner's title in German, speaking with a deliberate emphasis, "Standartenführer Meissner."

"Ah, I love that about our Japanese friends. A compliment is as good as an insult. And you, Liv, will you speak Japanese to me as well?"

"You know, sir, that she speaks English in the embassy," said Martin.

"Ah yes, the language of the enemy. But here in this room I suppose it is not a treasonous sign."

He sat on my desk, opened the top drawer and pulled out an old cloth-covered photo album that I kept in it.

"Do you mind?" he asked in English, opening the cover.

"Of course not."

"Is this you as a little girl?"

"Yes."

"Very pretty. Much too pretty to be wasted in a place like Japan."

"I don't understand."

"Never you mind," he said, snapping the cover shut, dropping the album in the drawer and shutting it with a flick of his wrist. "So, have you gathered any information for me concerning those members of the German community here in Tokyo who are exhibiting dubious attitudes towards our causes?"

"As you well know, sir," said Martin, standing up at his desk, "this is not our brief."

"Your brief?"

"Yes, sir. We translate documents that come to us in order to provide intelligence for Ambassador Stahmer. Our translations go directly..."

"I know where your translations go. Don't lecture me!"

"I'm sorry, sir. I didn't mean it like..."

"I don't care what you mean. I asked you two months ago, in November, to follow up on some leads which I provided for you. There are people in banking and commerce here and even perhaps diplomats attached to this very embassy who are not sufficiently loyal. I don't want another Sorge working here. It was that idiot Ott who allowed him access to everything, including his own wife. Helma, who was most fun loving, even went hiking with Sorge. I think they reached great heights together."

Meissner chuckled at his own quip. But then Martin made a remark that infuriated him.

"But sir, you yourself trusted Richard Sorge. You drank with him on many occasions, as I have heard from others. It was before I came to the embassy, of course."

"What in the hell do you mean by that, Stanczuk?! Are you accusing me of aiding and abetting a Soviet spy?"

Meissner walked over to Martin's desk and, leaning over it, buttoned his collar.

"Of course not, sir. I would never suggest such a thing. It's just that, as I have been told, you trusted him too. I was just commenting on how clever he..."

"But he wasn't clever, was he, Stanczuk? He got himself caught and thrown into prison. It's only a matter of time before they put a noose around the degenerate's neck and snap it."

He slowly turned his gaze from Martin to me.

"Now, let us not dwell on these dark matters," he said, tapping his fingernails on Martin's desk. "Keep up the good work, all of you. Remember, we even had a Jew working right here in the embassy until he was exposed. Ivar Lissner had made his way as an officer into the Abwehr, our military intelligence organ. Eugen Ott, that worm, didn't have the mettle to confront him but sent him packing to Manchuria instead. Of course, the Kempeitai got hold of him, once I informed them, and tortured him. I tell you, everything is changed now here. No more worms in our bodies. None whatsoever. We are cleansed."

"*Aa, sore wa anshin desu ne* (Well, that's a relief)," grinned

Inomata-san, still seated at his desk.

"And I have intelligence myself, you know, that two people in this room have decided to become man and wife," continued Meissner, ignoring Inomata-san's remark. "Stanczuk, Liv, are congratulations in order ... or is this still a state secret? Don't worry, I can keep a secret."

I didn't know how he found out that Martin and I had decided to marry. We had only discussed it between ourselves in the privacy of our bedroom. I suppose we should have realized that we would have no secrets from the likes of Donald Meissner. Even our bedroom was no longer a haven for us.

"Now, enough of these personal details. I want you to let me know if any information comes to you of a suspicious nature. You of all people are aware that there have been some minor setbacks in our march to victory. You should not disseminate any information that might cause our workers here in the embassy or our fellow countrymen in Japan dismay. You should pass on all facts to Ambassador Stahmer, but weed out anything of a pessimistic nature in your releases to others. Is that understood?"

"Yes sir," said Martin.

"Thank you and good morning. Heil Hitler."

Meissner clicked his heels together, saluted us and left the room. The information of a "pessimistic nature" that he had referred to had come to me through the short-wave radio that I listened to in the office. The BBC had announced that month—January 1944—that the Red Army had entered Poland, that the Allied Forces were making steady progress in southern Italy and that Berlin had been bombed. These "minor setbacks" were to turn into major defeats that year, as tens of thousands of German soldiers were killed in their retreat back to the Fatherland.

On Sunday I took the train to the city and went to David Jones, buying myself two new brightly coloured dresses for summer and a pair of white sandshoes. I wanted to create the picture of wholesome good cheer to the residents and staff of the Nola Road Nursing Home. I caught a bus to Glebe and popped into Gleebooks secondhand bookstore, spending $12.75 on a large and lavishly illustrated book, *The Eternal Art of Italy*. It was already nearly five o'clock. I was feeling tired and was waiting for the bus to Central when it struck me that Karen might be home. There was a red pay phone on the corner of Glebe Point Road and Parramatta Road. I rushed to it and inserted a ten-cent coin.

"Hello. This is Liv from the Nola Road Nursing Home. Is that Karen?"

"No, it's Jooles. Just a tick."

The bus pulled up to the stop.

"Hello?"

"Karen? It's Liv."

"Oh, hi."

"Look, I know it's ridiculously short notice but I happen to be in Glebe and, well, actually, I've got a book for you, so I thought ..."

"Sure. Great. Come on over. Now's a good time."

The block of flats was only a five-minute walk from the bus stop. It was a brick building with four storeys, not unlike the block that Karen's grandfather lived in. She was standing on the balcony of a top-storey flat when I arrived carrying the David Jones shopping bag into which I had slipped the book.

"Liv. Up here," she called, waving. "Sorry, no lift."

"That's all right," I said, pushing open the heavy cedar door.

"I'm afraid the place is a tip," she said as I entered.

"Oh, that's fine. No, it's very nice."

I looked around. Actually, her description had been accurate. The dishes and cups from lunch sat on a glass coffee table next to a pile of Dolly magazines, a copy of Nation Review and a soft-cover cookbook titled *Making Your Own Muesli*. On the floor was a half-eaten apple and, beside it, an overripe banana. Four bras hung from the antenna on top of the television. A tortoise shell cat was asleep on a crumpled heap of striped pyjamas.

"G'day, I'm Jooles," said a spunky-looking girl coming out of the bedroom. She wore tight denim shorts with a thin cowboy belt, a black skivvy and a leather jacket with an enormous zipper. "Just poppin' out."

She picked up the apple, took a bite and slipped the rest of it into her jacket pocket.

"When are you coming back, Jooles?" asked Karen.

"Oh I dunno. Sometime tomorrow maybe. Hey, Karen told me she met you at the home. I went there with her once. Geezus, was like a friggin' haunted house. Kinda freaked me out but. Met her granny too, but she was kinda out to lunch, y'know? What a bummer."

She went to the television and lifted a white lace-fringed bra off the antenna, then stepped over to the sofa and pulled the pyjamas from under the cat. The cat jumped up as if given an electric shock and made a beeline for the balcony.

"Sorry, Cuddles, the jammies're mine. Well, hooroo. See youse."

She pulled the apple out of her pocket and, holding it between her teeth, stuffed the bra into the same pocket, opened the door and left without shutting it. Cuddles took this as her chance to exit the flat too. She raced for the door and posed frozen on the landing, no doubt contemplating her options.

"Jooles's far out, isn't she? Sometimes she comes across as a bit over the top, but she's the most amazing person, I can tell you."

"I think so, though I must say I am not sure that I understood much of what she said. Was your grandmother out to lunch when she visited? If so, how did she meet her?"

"No," she said, removing the three bras from the antenna and picking up the blackened banana. "Sorry, this place is really a tip."

"Well, you are so busy at uni now, just finishing up before leaving the country."

"Busy? Lazy is more like it. And I can't get Jooles to lift a finger. We met when we were waitressing at this Lebanese place on Cleveland St. Jooles's part Lebanese, could you tell? She's got that swarthy complexion, which she hates, by the way. She rubs in some sort of alcohol thing or whatever it is to try to make her skin look whiter. But she does a mean belly dance, even though she doesn't really have the belly to go with it."

I still didn't know what "out to lunch" meant, but decided not to ask her again.

"Cuppa?"

"Yes, I'd love one."

"I've got coffee too. Bought some of that instant espresso at the deli."

"I'd love that. I've been out all day and am feeling a bit whacked, actually."

"Whacked? You have picked up the lingo, haven't you."

Tall bookshelves lined the wall on either side of the television. I was surprised to see such a wide variety of fiction and non-fiction ... novels by Flaubert and Balzac, Remarque's *All Quiet on the Western Front*, Dostoevsky's *Crime and Punishment*, short stories by Gogol, *Pride and Prejudice*, George Johnston's *My Brother Jack*, *A Spy in the House of Love* by Anais Nin; the poetry of Emily Dickinson and Judith Wright; books on Roman history, Bauhaus architecture and 1920s' fashion.

"You can borrow anything you like, Liv," she said, returning from the kitchen with a tray on which sat two coffees and a plate of Tim Tams.

"This doesn't look like regurgitation to me."

"Those books? No, those don't have anything to do with uni," she said, placing the tray on the glass coffee table. "It's sort of outside reading. Some of the books are Jooles's too. She doesn't look like it, but she's a voracious reader. She's really into feminist literature. She met Germaine Greer when she came to uni to give a talk. Germaine told her to leave Australia. Everybody has to leave this place to find himself. Australia is the middle of cultural nowhere. A Nullarbor of the mind, if you ask me. Sugar, milk?"

"Um, no thanks."

"Grandpa Dan gives me books. He really wants me to understand the outside world."

"Oh, which books? Which books did he give you?" I said, standing by the bookshelf to the right of the television.

"That whole shelf, just by your head."

"This one?"

"Yeah. That's all books I got from him, the Dostoevsky and that one about World War I."

"*All Quiet on the Western Front*?"

"Yeah. It's his favourite book. The Anais Nin and Emily Dickinson and things are Jooles's. She's a feminist."

I took the book on Italian art out of the shopping bag.

"I got this for you, Karen."

"Far out. You are so sweet, Liv. It's really what I wanted. In fact, Gleebooks, yeah, I saw this book there a couple of weeks ago. Couldn't afford it though."

"It's yours now."

"Thank you so much," she said, walking over to me and giving me a big hug.

"Look," I said, "it's too late for me to get home and make dinner. I saw what looks like a really nice Chinese restaurant across from the cinema. Shall we have a bite there? My treat, of course."

"Really. I've never been there before. Is it okay?"

"By all means," I said, taking a sip of the coffee and momentarily wincing. It was much too strong for me.

"Is it too strong?"

"No, it's perfect. Just like they make in Italy."

"I'll just go and put on something presentable," she said, undoing her ponytail.

She went into the bedroom. Cuddles re-entered the flat through the open front door and settled once again on the sofa. I sat next to her and stroked her, then returned to the bookshelves. There were some photographs in frames on the bookshelf to the left of the television. I picked one of them up. It was a black-and-white photograph of Karen when she was about seven or eight standing between her grandfather and grandmother in front of Ayers Rock.

"That's me with grandpa and grandma, like, twelve years ago or so," she said, returning to the room. "They took me to lots of places. Mum was kind of preoccupied with her own problems, I mean. The three of us went to the Jenolan Caves and, like, Adelaide when the festival was on and up to Cairns."

"That must have cost a lot of money," I said, replacing the photograph on the shelf.

"Oh, grandpa's loaded. He doesn't bother about money?"

"How did he get his money?"

"What? I don't know. In America. Well, I'm ready. I don't exactly look like Jooles, but these bell bottoms I got from Grace Bros. set me back a friggin' fortune."

It was nearly eleven when I got back to my flat in Gordon. Karen had asked me about my life and I told her that I had never been married, was childless and that my job was translating business papers and documents from Japanese into English. "Then why do you work, like, at nursing homes and stuff?" she asked. "To be charitable," I said. "To get closer to people."

I was racked by trepidation that night. The next day the man who now called himself Daniel Miles was bound to appear at the home in the late morning. I carried on an argument with myself in my head as to whether I should ignore him or engage him in a conversation. How could he possibly be so kind to his granddaughter, a man who had sent people to torture chambers and their deaths at the drop of a hat? How could he value a book like *All Quiet on the Western Front*, his "favourite book"? It was my favourite book too. That could not be possible! Its author had been vilified by the Nazis. They even executed his sister and sent their mother the bill for the funeral just to get back at him for leaving Germany and for writing about peace. I would have nothing in common with *that man*, not even a book!

I decided that I would cut my hair in the morning. I was unable to sleep. It was just three in the morning when I got out of bed, went into the bathroom and cut my long hair into an Egyptian bob, trimming it with a straight fringe in front.

"Well, Liv," I said to myself, nodding in front of the mirror. "If you didn't have those grey streaks you'd be mistaken for Elizabeth Taylor playing Cleopatra. Yeah, fat chance of that. More like Shirley Booth in *Come Back, Little Sheba*." It was a movie that had made me cry, about a precious little dog who ran away and never came back. That dog was the woman's own youth.

I washed the sink thoroughly, returned to bed and promptly fell asleep, not waking until half past eight. Once back in the bathroom I shook my pillow over the toilet to get the loose hairs off it, showered, shampooing myself thoroughly, and put on my new yellow sleeveless dress and a beige cardigan. It was already twenty-five degrees outside and a light breeze was blowing.

It was nearly ten when I arrived at the nursing home. The Asian nurse named Victoria was in the main room walking beside a very frail-looking wiry-haired man.

"Good morning. Is that Victoria?"

"Yes. I ..."

"Oh, I'm Liv. Remember? I stopped in last week."

"Yes, of course."

"I thought you were going to be away for ..."

"I came back early," she said, grimacing, as if something unpleasant had happened in Hong Kong.

"I've volunteered, actually," I said, smiling, quickly changing the subject. "Mrs. Archibold was kind enough to allow me to help out here. Look, I'll take Mr. ... uh, Mr. ..."

"Abbott."

"... Mr. Abbott to the loo. That's where he's going, isn't it?"

"Are you sure?"

"Absolutely. I'll have him back in two shakes of a lamb's tail."

I walked Mr. Abbott to the men's.

"Do you need any help, Mr. Abbott?" I asked, gently holding his elbow.

"Leave me alone. I can piss by myself, thank you very much. All you women here. You think a man's lost every facility. Treat us like bloody children, you do."

He opened the door to the men's, slamming it shut. He locked the door loudly for me to hear it. I could see the main room and the front door through the large rectangular glass panes of the French doors. As I was waiting for Mr. Abbott to emerge, the front door opened and *Donald* Miles entered the home, turning around to shut it. He walked slowly, using his stick, across the room, bowing and tipping his white Panama hat to Nurse Victoria, who smiled before rushing up the stairs to the residents' rooms. *Donald* Miles made his way across the room to the armchair that his wife Margaret was sitting in. Mr. Abbott opened the door of the men's.

"Are we finished?" I asked.

"Don't you patronize me!" he huffed, walking past me. "And

don't follow me. I know the way back to my place. Bloody hell."

I went to the kitchen, boiled the kettle and made myself a cup of tea, drinking it while drying the breakfast dishes that someone had washed. I had made my decision while dressing that morning that I was not going to speak to him. I would do that the next day. But I would observe him. Perhaps he would have retained some of his traits ... his unctuous politeness—always a mocking politeness—when he greeted you for the first time in the day ... his boorish manner when he engaged in conversation, gradually moving in on you with little shuffling steps until you could feel his breath all over your face ... his not-so-veiled warnings, generally couched in phrases of advice about how to deal with others, warnings that were really aimed at you. "That Japanese man—what's his name, Kuratani?—he calls himself a marquis. Pretentious Japanese *Schweinhund.* As if there could be nobility outside of Europe! He is making a fortune selling his blankets to the Japanese army and has offered to supply the Wehrmacht as well. To him war is money and opportunity for self-aggrandizement. Don't you think so, Martin? He is in this war for himself." That final comment was aimed directly at Martin. "And, Liv, dear dear Liv, our little Norwegian princess, did you know that Sorge was associating with your predecessor, Fräulein Barbara Viertel, also a potential Jewess, but we had her thoroughly checked out and she was Aryan? This sort of associating inside the embassy is not healthy, you know." That comment was directed at me. He put his arm around me and drew me to him, leading me into the corridor. "You must remain our little princess, Liv. I feel it my duty to look after you. Like a father."

A man who had been so close to me as to smother me with his breath ... and now I could see him through the thick panes of wavy glass, opening the drawers of the little table beside his wife's armchair, neatly arranging her things, kneeling at her feet and smoothing the wrinkles in her dress, and all along she just stares into the distance above his head unaware of who this man, acting in such a kind manner, is. I will tell you, Margaret. He is the ever-faithful Nazi with his Blood Order Medal who prides himself on prosecuting and torturing Jews and homosexuals, that's who he is. Is! This is your husband, Margaret Miles. Count yourself blessed that you have lost your memory. But you are not the only one, dear. Everyone has lost his memory. This country is one big nursing home with senile dementia. "Lest We Remember" ... that is the nation's motto. "Lest We Forget" is reserved for white Australians boys who were sent far away to fight in other people's wars. But not this little Norwegian princess. She remembers everyone. And she will make it her duty to revive the memory of others. Her duty.

"Excuse me, may I get through please?"

The daughter of one of the residents, a middle-aged woman dressed in a sari, was standing behind me. I was breathing heavily and gripping the knobs of the French doors tightly, as if hanging onto them over a gaping black hole below me.

"Oh, I'm sorry. I forgot myself for a moment."

"That's all right. You people work so hard here. I cannot thank you enough for looking after my mother."

"Oh, which one is she?"

"Well, it should be obvious, isn't it? The Indian lady standing in front of Mr. Abbott and trying to get him to drink his cup of tea. My mother thinks he is her husband."

I stepped aside and opened one of the French doors. The sweet smell of musk and sandalwood perfume came off her sari as she brushed by me.

Donald Miles was now not in the room. He couldn't have gone home so quickly. I went to where Nurse Victoria was standing. She was counting the number of residents present.

"Did you see Mr. Miles?" I asked. "Did he go somewhere?"

"Just a tick," she said, finishing her count. "Oh, that's a relief. I thought we had lost one of our residents. A few weeks ago Mrs. Lonergan just walked herself right out of here and no one noticed. Luckily we sew their names and our telephone number into all their articles of clothing. She was found wandering around Waltons in Chatswood. One of the managers there was sweet enough to drive her back. There he is. There's Mr. Miles. He's coming down the stairs. He must have gone up to his wife's room."

Nurse Victoria rushed to Mrs. Archibold's office, knocked on the door, opened it and went in. *Donald* Miles was walking towards me in the direction of his wife's armchair. Should I turn about and go to the kitchen? That's what I wanted to do. But for some reason I couldn't get my legs to move. I was frozen to the spot. He was now a mere four metres from me, walking slowly, gracefully lifting his stick in front of him and putting it down with each step. Then he was in front of me. He stared into my face. I lowered my gaze to the floor.

"Good morning," he said, touching the brim of his white hat.

He brushed by my arm. I instinctively pulled it in so that I would not feel any part of his body or clothing against me. I watched him from the back. He brought a folding chair from under the window to his wife's armchair, placed his hat on the side table and the shiny knob of his stick against it. He took a deck of cards from the side pocket of his jacket. He removed the plastic tray from the side table, put it over his knees and started to play Solitaire. He showed each card drawn to his wife, saying, "Look, Margaret, a seven of diamonds ... now where does that go? What's next, I wonder. Oh, a three of spades. And a king. Look, Margaret, a king. Maybe the next one will be a queen." Margaret seemed to delight in this game, though it was obvious that she didn't have a clue as to what the cards signified or for what purpose this strange man was playing with them in front of her.

He left not long after one. Once again I observed his every

move from the other side of the French doors. Mrs. Archibold came out of her office to say goodbye to him, shaking his hand vigorously and evidently thanking him for his daily visits. She opened the door for him and let him out, then caught my eye through the panes, squinting and grimacing, as if to say, "Why are you staring in this direction? Don't you have better things to do?"

I quickly walked up to her, catching her before she was able to enter her office.

"Mrs. Archibold, um, excuse me but I wonder if I might leave now."

"Of course, Liv. Not ill, I hope. We are so grateful to have you. Victoria's here and we're getting a new staff member this afternoon. Back tomorrow?"

"For sure. I'm fine, thank you."

It took me over an hour to get to St. Vincent's Hospital in Darlinghurst. It was not far from the Scottish Hospital where I had once volunteered.

"May I help you?" asked an elderly woman in a dress that showed dappled skin on her neck and ample cleavage below.

"Thank you. I've come to see a patient."

"The patient's name?"

"Ditzen. Mrs. Ditzen."

"Could you spell that?"

"Her surname? Her first name is ..."

"Yes, the surname," she said impatiently.

I spelled out Ditzen. She opened a large ledger-like volume and ran her finger down the margin to the letter D.

"Oh, Marlis. She's only a day out of surgery. Are you a relative?"

"Yes. I'm her, um, sister. Well, half-sister, really. We had the same father."

"Oh, Mr. Miles. Is he your father?"

"Well ... yes."

I had regretted saying this, but could come up with no other explanation that instant. I have never been clever when put on the spot. I have always required time to think up what would be my best excuse or most effective course of action in any circumstance.

"Such a wonderful man, your father! Those flowers are from him. He brought them yesterday. Very dapper too in his Panama hat and cravats. A different one every time. So European, he is, not at all like your Aussie blokes who saunter in here in shorts, a singlet and thongs. Sorry, I should have recognized the name. Room 54."

I knocked on the door. There was no answer. I let myself in. The private room was spacious and light. A television was mounted on a large metal bracket attached to the ceiling. Marlis Ditzen lay on the bed with a drip in her left arm.

"Excuse me for coming unannounced," I said. "I am a friend of Karen's. She told me about you. It just so happened that I was visiting a cousin who's also a patient here and I thought I would stop by. I had dinner with Karen just last night near her flat in Glebe."

"Thank you for coming," she said in a feeble voice, placing two fists onto the blanket and propping herself up. "Is she all right?"

"Oh yes, fine. We talked about Italy."

"Italy?"

I shouldn't have said that, I knew. Perhaps her mother was unaware that she was planning to go overseas. I suddenly changed the subject and spoke in a loud and enthusiastic voice.

"Jooles was there too. She's quite a young woman, isn't she."

"Jooles?" she snickered. "Yes she is. Has a heart of gold, though. Poor thing, she cried more when I told Karen about my hysterectomy than Karen did. She really feels for people, that girl."

"Did you have a hysterectomy?"

"Yes. Didn't Karen tell you?"

"No."

"Yep. Fallopian tubes, ovaries, the lot. May as well get it all once you're in there. You married?"

I was taken aback by her sudden question.

"No."

"Children?"

"No. … But I had one once."

"Oh dear. I'm sorry."

I don't know why I told her that. Perhaps I was subconsciously trying to make her feel sorry for me by ingratiating myself with her.

"I was very young," I said.

She leaned back, made a face and said, "Oooo."

"Are you okay?"

"Yes. Just a twinge. So, how did you meet my daughter?"

"I volunteer at the nursing home where …"

"… where my mother is?"

"Yes. In Roseville."

"Volunteer? I didn't know anybody did anything for free anymore. Money, money, money. That's the only thing that motivates people these days. Well, I'm just as bad. This hospital room is costing an arm and a leg. But my father is paying for it. So I'm just like everybody else. No different. Even my ex-husband. He choofed off to Nimbin and you'd think he was just a middle-aged hippie with his long hair, beard and beads around his neck, you know, make love not war, but he really went up there to make cheese. He formed a company. The motto of his company is, Find Your Own Whey."

"Where's Nimbin?"

"Oh, way up north. It's a kind of hippie community. But he didn't go for the free love either. That sort of thing was never his forte, not with me anyway. He got this idea in his head to make cheese and market it. You know, organic, alternative, whatever you call it. Oh, he did go in the company of a female, the daughter of a Chilean politician in Allende's government who migrated here after the coup. Oooo, another twinge. That hurt."

"Shall I call a doctor?"

"No, I'll be fine. So, I both gained and lost a husband thanks to immigration. First mine, then hers. What you lose on the swings you also lose on the roundabouts. Story of my life, really."

"Karen is lovely."

"Think so? She hasn't found herself yet. When I was twenty, you either knew who you were or you didn't. We didn't have the luxury of indecision."

"Give her time."

"Yeah. Time. People don't always have as much as they think they do though."

She peered into my face when she said that, as if her words had been directed specifically at me. A nurse holding a clipboard entered the room.

"I think I had better be going," I said, standing.

"Thank you so much for coming. You know, I didn't get your name. You have an accent, a nice one."

"Liv. Liv Bang."

"Bang as in B-A-N-G?"

"Yes. It's a normal Norwegian name. Even a good one. But I don't use it here in Australia. I use my mother's maiden name. Grimstad."

"Why not? Oh I guess I can see why. Aussies have a pretty raunchy sense of humour. You'd definitely get ribbed about it. I lost my accent because I had to. When I arrived here in the fifties with mum and dad I was already in my twenties. If anything I had an American accent, which was worse then than having a European one. But I soon learned that I would have a hard time if I sounded like a Yank or what people called a 'reffo.' Things are better here now. Sometimes I think there are more new Australians than old ones."

"I did use Bang, my father's name, actually, in my first years here. That's why I switched. Too much flak. Not so different from you."

This was the first time in years I had told anyone my real name. Was I opening up to this family naturally? Why did I feel at such ease with them? I would have to fight against this emotion inside myself. I would have to act objective and seemingly aloof when I fronted up to the man who brought this family into this world.

Instead of going straight home I took a detour to the large nature reserve in St. Ives. The dense stands of blackbutt and blue gum eucalyptuses were among the last vestiges of Sydney's native forests, the descendants of the trees that Capt. Cook and his men would have seen two hundred years ago. The tops of the blue gums, broad fans of leaves, were swaying back and forth in the wind. I wound my way on the path by giant ferns and stopped before one that hung over me like a fine Japanese umbrella. A king parrot, bright red except for a cape of green covering its back, was perched on one of the thicker fronds that was seesawing from the movement of its body. Suddenly I heard the laughing call of a kookaburra. But when I looked in its direction I saw a lyre bird prancing around a blueberry lily bush, opening and shutting its beak in the mimicking call. "That's a talent I wish I had," I said to myself, "sounding convincingly like someone entirely different from myself." The leaf-curling spider that had connected its web from a fern frond to the trunk caught my eye. Only the tips of its legs were visible at the edge of the cone-like home it had made for itself out of a leaf. She was waiting patiently for her prey to come along. She would not leave the safety of the leaf curled in on herself before her prey came near her. Ah, I thought, moving on and now anxious to get home, it's not healthy when a woman starts seeing herself everywhere in nature. Don't keep questioning your motives and actions, Liv. Just act naturally. But what did it mean to "act naturally"? Martin had told me, "Take every day as it comes," and that was a time when no one knew the number of days remaining to him. This was not 1945 in Japan or Germany or any other country in Asia or Europe. It was 1975 in Australia, a country where people came to put their past behind them once and for all, where it presumably didn't matter where you came from and what you, your parents or grandparents had done elsewhere. Leaving was as good as forgetting, being there as good as being forgiven.

That walk did me the world of good. It also transported me back to my childhood in Moji and reminded me of the one trip we took by ship from Japan to Norway in 1931, when I was eleven. We visited my grandparents' farm in the mountains outside Trondheim. Granddad was convalescing from a tractor accident. He had driven the tractor too far up the steep rocky slope behind the house and it just flipped over. Luckily it hadn't landed on top of him, and all that he had suffered was a slipped disk in his back. "Working the farms up here has never been easy," he said, stroking my hair as I sat on the bed beside him. "Making a living here is like walking a tightrope every day." It was coming up to Christmas, and granny was taking fillets of cod out of a bowl of water. "What's that smell, granny?" I asked her. "Lye. It's *lutefisk*. I've cured the cod in water and lye." I had been used to eating raw fish in Japan so it didn't bother me that the fish hadn't been cooked. But the acrid smell of lye stayed with me. I don't remember much else of my trip "home" except for getting out of bed in the middle of the night, going to the window and seeing the moonlight, as thick as marmalade, reflected on the soft sheet of snow covering the slopes behind the house. So whenever I was asked by Australians where I came from, I felt that I could hardly say "Norway," having spent only two months there. If I said

"Japan" everyone came back with a similar comment—"You don't look Japanese!" I didn't have a country to come from. Perhaps that was not something to regret. Perhaps it was a saving grace.

Martin and I went to sleep early on the night of the 9th of March, 1945. Besides the ambassador, who was personally briefed by Martin, we two and Inomata-san were the only people in the embassy who knew how dire the situation was for Germany and Japan. Churchill, Roosevelt and Stalin had met at Yalta in the Crimea, setting out the terms of the postwar order. The old city of Dresden had been firebombed, killing tens of thousands of people, many of them German and non-German refugees forced from the land by the advance of the Red Army. The American forces were attacking Iwo Jima in a battle that was decimating the Japanese troops.

"We must start planning our escape, Liv," said Martin to me after we made love.

I put my finger up to my lips.

"Nothing to worry about. They have better things to do now than to listen to what we tell each other. The embassy is in a state of controlled chaos. It will only take one spark to ignite a fire that unleashes that chaos. It's then that we have to escape."

"But where can we go?" I said, putting my arm over his chest and kissing his neck. The smell of his neck is something I will never forget.

"Didn't you say that your parents used to go up to Lake Nojiri in Nagano during the summer months, to get away from the heat?"

"Yes. But they didn't have their own house there. They stayed in a kind of communal cottage or hut that was built by Dr. Winther, a Danish missionary way back at the time of the Russo-Japanese war."

"If we went there we might be able to stay or maybe someone would put us up, find room for us," he said. "We could pack a lot of food that's stored in the embassy basement and take it with us. They've got hams there and all sorts of preserved fruits and vegetables, not to mention sacks of rice and cases of liquor."

"How would we get there? If we went by train we'd be spotted and stopped by the police, at least for questioning. You can't be in possession of so much food now. It all has to go to the army."

"Yeah, right. But Inomata-san has a car that he drives every day to the embassy from his home at Soshigaya Okura. He might lend it to us, I mean, go up there with us and then drive back. He's a Japanese and because he works at the German embassy he's got impeccable papers."

"When would we do it, Martin? I'm scared."

I sat up in bed. Martin leaned towards me.

"You are so beautiful, my little Norwegian ..."

"Don't you dare call me a princess. That's what he calls me."

"I wasn't going to say 'princess.' I was going to say 'sugar snail.'"

"Sugar snail? I haven't heard that one before."

"Well, it sounds a lot better in German. You see, there are distinct disadvantages in speaking the enemy's language to the woman you love."

He started kissing my breasts, then my stomach. "I do love you, Liv Bang," he said. "I love you more than life itself."

"Shh, Martin," I said, taking his head in my hands and pointing to the ceiling and then all around the room.

"Let them hear it. Actually, they probably are listening now. Let the world know how much I love you."

We were awakened a couple of hours later by the sound of bombs whistling in the air and thunderous explosions a few kilometres away. We could see a red glow coming through the flimsy curtains over the window facing the river and the downtown districts across from it.

"The Americans are bombing Tokyo," said Martin, rushing to the window and looking out. "It's finally started, the beginning of the end."

"Martin, get away from the window!"

"It's all right. It's not happening right here. But, Liv, I've got to get to the embassy."

"The embassy? It's—what time is it?—it's just after midnight, Martin."

"But people will be there. I've got to make sure all my papers are in the safe, just in case something happens to the guards and the embassy ceases to be secure."

"But something could happen to you."

Both of us were standing naked in the room that was now itself faintly glowing in red. Our bodies looked like there was a red light inside them. The acrid smell of smoke had made its way into the room. Martin parted the curtains and peeked out.

"It's a massive firebomb attack. Must be cluster bombs. And from the smell, which is like petrol, it's probably napalm that they're using."

He rushed to the chest of drawers and took out underclothes.

"I'm going too," I said.

"Don't be ridiculous, Liv. It's dangerous out there."

"I don't care. I have a job to do too."

"A job? For Germany? What Germany? There is no more Germany now, Liv. It's kaput, finished, gone to hell. The little patch of German soil that the embassy is on is eventually going to be scorched to the earth. It will survive only as the burnt soil of Germany so far away from its home. Wherever there is a little corner of Germany, it's going to be destroyed and burnt to the ground. No distance is safe."

"I don't care. I want to be with you, Martin."

"Where's my wallet," he said. "I may need to show my papers if someone stops me."

I had slipped a dress on and was pulling woolen tights over my legs.

"There, on the floor by the leg of the bed."

"Right. Now, you stay. You could get burned alive, Liv, and for what?"

"I'm going with you, Martin. I want to be with you tonight. Nothing is going to separate us. Nothing."

The embassy was only a twenty-minute walk away. That part of the city was not being bombed, yet there was almost no one on the streets. Large embers like blackened sheets of crepe were floating above our heads. It looked as if sparks were racing through the air, torching hundreds of Japanese kites in the sky.

When we reached the embassy many of the people who worked there were rushing about. They had taken to staying nights at the embassy rather than make the journey home after work. I noticed Inomata-san's car, a Chrysler sedan built in Japan, parked on the side of the building. He too had evidently stayed the night in the embassy.

Martin ran through the front door and bounded up the stairs. I was about to follow him when I caught sight of a barefoot little Japanese girl in a green dress standing next to a marble pillar by the door. I went up to her, knelt in front of her and spoke to her in Japanese. I had never seen her in the embassy before.

"Hello. What's your name? How old are you?"

After a long pause she put a finger up to her cheek and said, "My name is Minako. I am ten years old. I am going to turn eleven in August, however."

I could tell by her use of polite language that she came from an educated family.

"Does your father or mother work here?"

"No."

"I see. Come over here. Let's sit on this bench for a minute."

I led her inside to a marble bench on the edge of the rotunda. More people were entering the embassy. I saw Donald Meissner, in full uniform, stride in and go up to the second floor, taking three steps at a time.

"How did you get here?"

"I was with my mummy. In our car. She was driving me. But when the bombs started to fall she said she had to go back to aunty's because that's where she left my little brother and sister."

"Where did she go?"

"That way."

She pointed to the river and downtown Tokyo where the bombs were falling.

"She told me to get out. I didn't want to though. She stopped the car outside. She said I would be safe in this building, to go inside and not leave until she came back."

Minako started to cry. I hugged her. She sobbed, her entire body shaking in my embrace.

"Now, Minako-san, listen to me. My name is Liv. Can you say that?"

"Liv."

"Good. Come upstairs with me."

"But mummy said to stay here."

"I'm sure that she meant to stay in the building. You'll be safe upstairs. I'll be with you until your mummy comes back."

I put my arms down, letting go of her. Minako gradually stopped crying and placed her hand in my palm.

When we got to the room, Martin and Inomata-san were going through papers, stuffing some of them in the large safe in the corner and discarding others in the rubbish bins. I sat Minako in a chair beside the safe and handed her an apple that I had kept in my desk drawer.

"I smell smoke," I said.

A tall German woman in evening dress, white gloves and high heel shoes was carrying a metal box with a fire burning in it down the corridor.

"What's going on?" I asked.

"Oh, Bang-san," said Inomata-san, "our friend from the Gestapo is attempting to cover some of his tracks. He must think that time is running out."

"But there is no fire here. What is he doing? This isn't an attack on the embassy. It's an attack on the city of Tokyo, the people of Tokyo."

"Yes, you are right. But some people here are worried, Bang-san. They are thinking not of their past but of their future. Some papers set people free, other papers incriminate them."

I stood in the door of our room. The German woman had simply taken the box to the embassy's side window, opened it and dumped the contents out, fire and all. She was returning with an empty smouldering box. I stepped out of the room and stood in front of her.

"Get out of my way!" she shouted.

"What in hell do you think you're doing? You could start a fire here."

"It's none of your business. Let go of the box. You'll burn your pretty little hands."

I was incensed. Though it wasn't in my nature to openly challenge people, I felt that I was not going to let these people endanger my life any more than they had already.

"Put down this box, *Schlampe* (Slut)!" I screamed in her face. It wasn't exactly the proper word for her at that time and place, but it was the only German swearword that I knew.

She carefully placed the metal box at my feet, stared into my eyes and slapped me hard across the face. Then she said something in what sounded like a German dialect that I didn't understand. Minako, who had been watching the confrontation from the doorway, came up to me and stood behind me, grasping the folds of my dress. Just then Donald Meissner, now without his jacket, approached from behind carrying another large metal box. Flames rose from the box as he held it away from his body.

"Get out of my way. What are you doing here? Who asked you to come here? Move!" he shouted.

He took a step to the side in order to go past me, but slipped on the stone floor, dropping the box. It landed on its side. Flames and burning paper shot out from the box, sending sparks into the air. Sparks struck Minako's dress. She screamed, took a breath, then screamed again. The sparks had already jumped from the hem of her dress to the smocking across her chest. She fell to the floor, lying on her back. I immediately put my body on top of her and embraced her tightly. This put out the flame. A tongue of dark-grey smoke rose into the air from between our bodies.

"Are you all right?" I said, frantically.

She appeared to be in shock, staring up at me with wide-open eyes. I looked over her dress and ran my hand down it. It had burned away in places. Miraculously her skin, though blackened by smoke, was unscathed.

"Now get out of this corridor," hollered Donald Meissner, turning around mechanically, as a soldier does an about-face, and marching back to his office. The German woman in high heels was not there. I had not seen her go. But just as I was helping Minako up, the woman returned with another metal box, this time a smaller one, with its contents on fire. She walked by us as if we didn't exist.

We stayed at the embassy until morning. It seemed that the entire downtown area, where the working people of Tokyo lived, had been destroyed in one night. I had made a bed for Minako out of a large striped rya rug that I had brought back to Japan from Trondheim when I was little. I slept in my chair, with my head on my desk. When I awoke a few minutes past seven Martin was chatting with Inomata-san by the closed safe. They were speaking in whispers, but I caught the word "automobile." Inomata-san nodded and they shook hands. It looked as if Martin was putting the final details together for our escape to the mountains of Nagano. "We'll wait out this war there," he had told me as we were falling asleep the night before. "Whatever happens … however long it takes … you and I will be together. We will look back at all this in the way we recall a nightmare. The fact that we witnessed and shared a nightmare will remain with us. But the details will fade away. All in good time, Liv, all in good time…."

Those were the words I recalled as I fell asleep in my Sydney flat. But I was attaching a different meaning to them. Over and over I said to myself, "I will make you relive the nightmare, Donald Meissner … and, for once, I will do it all in my own good time." Those words repeating—"in *my own* good time, in my own good time"—were like an incantation, an incantation that sent me, for once in more than half a lifetime, into a peaceful and dreamless sleep.

The next day I left my flat at eight-twenty and walked to Gordon Station to take the train to Roseville. When we were pulling into Killara Station I caught sight of Mrs. Barnes on the platform. She was dressed in black with a pearl necklace and was carrying a black parasol. The car I was travelling in passed her just before the train stopped. I quickly rose and left the car, walking towards the back of the train.

"Mrs. Barnes, Mrs. Barnes," I said, waving.

She briefly looked in my direction, squinting from the sunlight and seemingly not recognizing me. When I was beside her we entered the train together.

"It's Liv. I visited you, remember? The lady from the park?

With the rhubarb cake?"

"Of course I do. How have you been, dear?"

We sat side-by-side. Two teenage girls in matching banana-yellow jumpsuits and platform shoes with thick cork soles stood directly in front of us.

"I've been fine, thank you," I said. "I've come to know Mr. Miles, the man who lives opposite you."

"Oh, Mr. Miles!" she said with a big smile, tapping my knee with her fingertip. "Such an angel, he is. Last year Jack, that's my husband, awoke in the middle of the night and he couldn't catch his breath, you know, well, wheezing and gagging for breath, you know. I didn't know what to do so I knocked on his door. It was three in the morning, mind you, but he came immediately and insisted on driving Jack to the Mater."

"The Mater?"

"Yes, the Mater Hospital in North Sydney."

The train stopped at Lindfield Station and the girls in front of us, who had spent the minutes closely examining each other's split ends, got off.

"I have never met a more selfless man than Daniel Miles. We, that's Jack and I, go to the St. John's Church in Gordon, and I tell you, you don't find many there who have the genuine Christian spirit as he does. We became friends after that, well not exactly friends but acquaintances, that's the word I was looking for. He visits his poor wife every day. She's lost her marbles, you know, poor dear. Hasn't a clue who he is. But he persists. He persists. He's not the kind of man who gives up, your Mr. Miles."

We sat in silence as the train pulled into Roseville Station.

"Well, this is where I get off," I said.

"Do come and see us, Liv. I think that Jack is quite taken with you. We'll invite Mr. Miles over and make it a foursome."

"Thank you, Mrs. Barnes. Goodbye."

"Goodbye, dear."

I crossed the Pacific Highway and walked towards Maclaurin Parade. There was a crowd of about thirty men of ages ranging from their twenties to their nineties standing outside the RSL Club.

"G'day, darl," said one of the older men, lifting his hat off his head. "Where ya off to in such a hurry?"

It was already sweltering, and beads of sweat had formed on my forehead.

"Hello," I said, walking past the men.

"Don't rush off, darl. We're waitin' for the club to open. Tomorrow's the big day, y'know."

I stopped and turned around.

"Remembrance Day," he continued. "Some of us blokes here fought in the Great War, y'know. We got the Somme here, and Passchendaele, and Bert over there was at Wipers...."

I didn't know what to say, so I just stood there smiling.

"Josh here's the youngest. Lost a leg for his country in Vietnam, he did."

He pointed to a young man, who, with a face full of pimples, looked no older than a teenager. He wore dark-grey trousers and scuffed black leather shoes. You could not tell which leg he had lost.

The door to the club opened and the men filed inside. The old man looked back at me.

"See ya 'round," he said, crinkling his eyes.

I walked down the hill and turned into Nola Road, stopping to blot my forehead and the back of my neck with a handkerchief.

It was nearing noon by the time we were able to make it home from the embassy. Mrs. Yoshida had gone somewhere and was not to return. We were all alone in the lodging house. The firebombing of Tokyo in the early hours of March 10th had paralyzed the city. We were all ordered to leave the embassy and not return until given notice to do so. I had no choice but to bring Minako home with me. I immediately tried to phone her home, to let her mother know that she was safe, but the line was dead.

"Do you know the number at your aunty's," I asked.

"No."

"Do you know the address where they live?"

"It's in Asakusa."

"Ah, that whole area …"

I was about to tell her that Asakusa was burnt to the ground, but of course such a thing would have terrified her. Why did it even cross my mind to ask where her aunty lived, knowing that there was nothing but ash left beyond the other bank of the river where she had pointed to? I was dead tired and numb after having to listen to the orders of *that man.*

"You will be safe here, Minako-san. I will look after you."

"Are you a Japanese?" she asked, cocking her head.

"No. Does that matter?"

"I don't think so."

"He's Martin. He doesn't speak Japanese very well. We speak English together. Do you know any English?"

"No. They don't let us learn English at school."

"Of course. Well, don't worry. I was born in Japan and have spent my life here. I was here when I was your age too, so I know just how you feel. Would you like something to eat?"

"Yes, please. Do you mind if I sit down?"

"Of course not."

She sat on the sofa, put her head on its arm and, in less than ten seconds, was out like a light.

"What are we going to do, Martin?" I said, holding my body against his and wrapping my arms around his waist.

"Leave, that's what we're going to do. Inomata-san said he would drive us to Nagano whenever it suited us. I told him we would be leaving soon. I just need to get back to the embassy once to pick up some things. I want to have certain papers with me when the Americans invade Japan. I may die along with everyone else. But if I don't and I have those papers, I can prove that you and I were doing our best, however little it was, to block the links between German and Japanese intelligence. The papers are in the safe. Not even Donald Meissner knows the combination."

"But we're not allowed in the embassy yet."

"I'll go back tomorrow. Today the military guards will still be there. By tomorrow things will have eased, and some of the embassy guards will no doubt have been called away to help clean up after the fires and sort out bodies for the Japanese."

"But it's dangerous, Martin. Don't go. We can hold out here for a few weeks. I've stored up food. Minako will be safe here too until we get her back to her mother, eventually."

"Ow, Liv, you're hurting me. I can't breathe."

I was hugging him tightly with muscles so tense that my arms were shaking. I dropped my arms to my sides and suddenly felt faint. Martin embraced me, holding my limp body up.

"Sit down, sweetheart. You're at the end of your tether. I don't blame you. You should never have had to go through all this."

"It's all because I'm Norwegian. We're Germany's friends now, so we're in the same boat. But the war will end. Everything has an end except a sausage."

"What?"

"A sausage has two ends. It's a Norwegian proverb my father taught me."

I had said this in all seriousness, but for some reason Martin had found my words terribly funny and started to giggle. Though I had had nothing to drink, I felt tipsy and lightheaded. I started giggling, too, then yawned and inhaled deeply.

"You're overtired, sweetheart. This war is asking too much of you. Sit here, next to Minako. Shh. That's right. Lean back. Listen, things are turning our way. I've seen the intelligence. The British and the Soviets are making inroads into Norway. It's only a matter of time before Norway falls back into Allied hands, though some say that Hitler won't give up Norway without scorching its earth. If he can't have it, no one will."

"And I haven't ever been there really, except once. How can you 'be' from a country you don't know? Perhaps the next time I get there it won't be there at all."

I stretched out my hand to touch Minako, who was fast asleep beside me.

"Shh. It's time for you to sleep too, my love. Leave everything to me. Just leave everything to me. Before you know it we will be living in some old wooden hut beside that lake where, you said, the water is freezing even in summer."

"Yes … freezing. I remember going there as a child in the summer. A sausage does have two ends, doesn't it, Martin? I mean, you could consider one of its ends as a beginning." I was trying as hard as I could to explain it to him, but yawned again, straining to think as clearly as I could. I shut my eyes.

"Your skin gets bumps as big as cloudberries when you jump in … in the … in the, um, lake," I said, my voice tapering off to a whisper. "My parents once told me that it …"

That's the last thing I remember saying before an immense wave of sleep washed over me. When I awoke I was alone on the sofa. The old wall clock said eleven-forty. Below its face was an advertisement for the sweet milk-like drink, Calpis—"One glass of Calpis has the taste of first love." Neither Minako nor Martin was in the room. I rose and went to the kitchen. Minako was seated at the table eating a hard-boiled egg.

"I saw two eggs in the cupboard so I boiled them. I hope that's all right," she said.

"It's wonderful that you can make your own breakfast. When I was your age I couldn't even boil an egg."

"Well, it's all I can do too."

She smiled at me. It was the first time I saw her smile.

"Don't worry, Minako-san, we'll find your mother," I said, kneeling beside her.

"I telephoned her there, from the telephone in the corridor," she said, pointing. "It was too high. I stood on a mandarin orange crate. I put it back, though."

"The phones are out because of the fires. The bombs must have destroyed the exchange."

"The phone rang. It just rang and rang."

"Oh, in that case the phones must be working again. We'll get through. I'll keep trying for you. Did you see Martin?"

"Yes. He left a long time ago."

"A long time ago?"

"Well, I don't know how long. I woke up. He was still here then. He made himself a cup of coffee. Then he left."

"Did he say where he was going?"

"No."

"All right. Now please listen carefully, Minako-san."

"I will."

"I am going to find Martin. I think I know where he is. You must stay here. Do not try to leave and find your mother. The streets are not safe yet. There are lots of cars racing about and *furosha* (stragglers)."

"What's *furosha*?"

"Um, people who, um, just wander about and don't know where to go."

"Am I a *furosha*?"

"No, of course not. You have a mother and a home. And I am going to look after you until you are where you belong."

She smiled again, this time more faintly.

"I'll wait here."

"Promise?"

"Yes."

I stuck out the pinkie of my right hand. She hooked her pinkie onto it and we pumped our hands up and down three times.

"All right, it's a promise now."

I went to the toilet, then washed my face, combed out my hair, which reeked of smoke, and left for the embassy. The building looked deserted from the outside. But Inomata-san's Chrysler was still parked where it had been before. I entered the building. There was no one in the rotunda. I climbed the stairs to the second floor. Again, no one to be seen. I went to our room. The lights were on. Donald Meissner was standing alone, with his back to the door, beside the open safe. He must have heard me enter. He snapped his head around and glared at me.

"He's not here, if that's why you came."

"Where is he? We were at home."

"Yes, I know."

"Where is Martin?"

"Just go home now. You have no reason to be here today."

"Where is Martin!" I screamed.

He walked leisurely to the window and looked out to the building across the street.

"Stanczuk has been taken away."

"Taken away?"

"Yes, by the authorities."

He now turned his body towards me and walked up to me. Though his face was only centimetres away from mine, I stared back into his eyes.

"What authorities?"

"The Japanese authorities, needless to say. There are no other authorities in this country. The Kempeitai. The military police."

"Why? He has broken no laws."

"Laws?"

He chuckled, laying his left palm on my shoulder. I momentarily stooped and walked past him.

"Where is he? I am going to see him."

"That's not possible, Fräulein Bang. I called them in when I caught him stealing documents from the safe here. I spent …"

"He wasn't stealing!"

"Shut up! The papers here belong to the German Reich. Now, as I was saying, I spent the night in the embassy. Alone. Even Ambassador Stahmer was too afraid to stay. One has to show one's mettle, Fräulein Bang, not just talk it up. I heard someone come. It was your fiancé, or whatever he is. Yes, of course we have known all along. Oh, it doesn't matter. We expect this sort of thing. And here I had thought that Stanczuk was a homosexual. He has that, well, manner."

Meissner picked up his jacket that was draped over my desk and took a packet of cigarettes out of its inside pocket.

"Smoke?"

I didn't answer. I stood by the window with my back to him.

"Turn around, Liv."

"Don't use my first name," I said, still not facing him.

"He will be in for questioning, nothing else. They will no doubt let him go in a few days or weeks, once they satisfy themselves that he was not going to use those papers for some sinister purpose. After all, there are some Japanese names on them. He said that he only wanted to take them home to keep them safe. Who knows, perhaps they will believe him? They are very naïve, the Japanese military police. Soft at heart. He should consider himself lucky that he was not detained by our people in Germany. They would immediately apprehend you, his lover, and torture you in front of him. How long would a man like him hold out then?"

"Then why did you come to Japan?" I said, turning around

and looking him straight in the eye. "You would be much more at home among your own kind, wouldn't you, Herr Meissner? The kind that torture innocent women in front of their lovers. The kind that denounce and denounce and denounce others in order to make themselves look good and shine in front of their superiors. The kind that take delight in witnessing the pain of others? Don't you have a word for it, Herr Meissner? Isn't it *Schadenfreude*? Oh, pardon my pronunciation. I may be an Aryan, as you call them, but I am not German."

"You have misread me," he said, sitting on my desk.

"No, Herr Meissner, I have read you like a book. You should go back to your Fatherland as soon as possible. I would think you'd be in your element in such a place. Do you understand that English turn of phrase, Herr Meissner? To be in your element?"

"You're right, Fräulein Bang. I would prefer to be among my own. But by my own I mean not only Germans, but Europeans, like you. I don't feel comfortable with these obsequious little people, always bowing like puppets on a string, sucking in their saliva, shaking hands as if holding a dead fish. I love you Norwegians, Fräulein Bang and ..."

"I am not one of 'your' Norwegians! I consider myself one of your little obsequious puppets, a Japanese."

"You may consider yourself so, but you are not so and you will never be, not in their eyes. The Norwegians are true Aryans, as you rightly say. We have so much to share. I am enamoured of your literature ... Bjornson, Hamsun. Do you know that Knut Hamsun gave his Nobel Prize for Literature medal personally to Minister of Public Enlightenment and Propaganda Goebbels? What a noble gesture, don't you think? Now, calm down and stop glaring at me like that. You look like the person in Edvard Munch's 'The Scream,' only with your lips shut. You can't scream with your lips shut, Fräulein Bang. If you want to, open up your lips and scream. Be my guest.

There's no one here. It will do you the world of good. Don't spend your life holding back a scream. Let go of yourself, Liv Bang, let go."

I paused and spoke softly, barely able to contain my anger.

"Where is Martin? I will go and see him."

"You want to see him?" he said, rising, tossing the unlit cigarette onto my desk and approaching me. "That might be arranged. Did Richard Sorge try to sleep with you?"

"What?!"

"You heard me correctly. Helma Ott, the ambassador's wife, could hardly satisfy a man like that. He was a terror, you know. I can't believe that he never at least tried. You are very beautiful, Liv."

He was now standing right in front of me, leering down at me. My back was touching the velvet curtains.

"Get away from me right now," I said, looking into his cornflower-blue eyes, those eyes that I would never forget. "Your foul breath is like shit coming out of your mouth."

"Oh dear, such a little princess and such filthy language, as one hears from a prostitute or a Bavarian farm girl. Well, I think I am being given—how do you call it?—the cold shoulder? Ah yes, I never had the charm of your Richard Sorge. At any rate," he sighed, walking over to the safe and slamming it shut, "I will keep under consideration charging Martin Stanczuk under German law as well, which is perfectly within my jurisdiction at this embassy, which I remind you is on German soil, seeing as he is a German citizen, unlike you who are merely a citizen of an occupied nation."

"You can't charge him with anything. What, stealing documents which he had a perfect right to look after?"

"No, the documents are insignificant. Do you think that the ambassador and I do not know what is in them? We are aware of the true situation much more keenly and thoroughly than you are, Fräulein Bang. The ambassador may not know it, but I am sure that Germany will be defeated and much sooner than anyone here imagines. We must be prepared. But until that time, the law must be obeyed."

"What law?"

"The law of 1934 according to the Act for the Prevention of Hereditary Diseases. You see, your fiancé can be sterilized if found guilty. Stanczuk is obviously a misfit, which makes him mentally incapable of being a law-abiding citizen. Thousands have been sterilized in Germany for much less serious transgressions than those he has demonstrated here in the embassy. But look, I do not wish to threaten you. Go back home to your little Japanese girl. I will help you locate her family. We can call in the Kempeitai."

"Leave them out of this. I will find the girl's mother myself."

"Ah, Fräulein Bang, you are so—what is the Japanese word?—*takumashii*? Doesn't that mean 'resilient'? You will bounce back. Once this war is over you will go back to your country or somewhere and bounce right back. Like a little white pingpong ball that has been struck in one direction then another, and then finally let loose into the air."

He picked up his jacket, turned his back to me and walked out. I knew that Martin had kept a luger in the safe. I ran to it. I would grab it, go to the corridor and shoot Donald Meissner in the back. There would be no one to witness this act. I would wipe the luger's handle of my fingerprints, replace it in the safe and walk out. I would contact the Kempeitai myself and find out where Martin was. He would be set free and we would escape to Nagano in Inomata-san's car, waiting out the war by the lake with the freezing-cold water. But the safe had automatically locked when slammed shut. I couldn't get to the luger. I plopped down at my desk and ran my forearm over it where his jacket had been, as if this motion alone would be sufficient to rid my presence of his every trace.

I arrived back home in the early afternoon. Minako was

not there. I called out her name everywhere in front of and behind the building. I asked passersby if they had seen a little girl in a light-green dress with burnt patches in it. I went to the neighbourhood police box. Again, no sighting of a little girl in a green dress. I asked the young policeman to record her as a missing person, but he seemed to be taking much more of an interest in me than in her. I told him that I was a German national working at the German embassy and this seemed to satisfy him. He saluted me and disappeared into the box.

After reaching home I phoned Minako's mother every fifteen minutes until late in the evening. I steamed myself some unpolished rice and boiled two small sweet potatoes. I switched on the radio. The news announcer reported that one hundred thousand people, perhaps more, had been killed in the fires of the early morning, fires that were still burning in the narrow streets lined with old wooden houses in the low-lying districts of downtown Tokyo. People interviewed on the radio called Americans "beasts," "inhuman cold-blooded murderers" and "war criminals who deserve to die, down to the very last man." The phone rang and I rushed to the corridor where it was attached to the wall.

"Martin?" I said frantically, putting the receiver to my ear.

"*Moshi moshi, Bangu-san*? (Hello, Miss Bang?)"

"Oh, Inomata-san."

"I'm sorry to phone so late. Are you coming to the embassy tomorrow?"

"Should I? I thought that we should be staying away until all the fires were out in the city."

"The embassy building is not in danger. Please come. Ambassador Stahmer is going to address the staff. You should be there too. After that, we can make … the necessary arrangements. Do you understand my meaning?"

"Yes, I do, thank you, Inomata-san. I am so grateful to you."

"I am so grateful to you, Bang-san, for coming to my

country and loving it so much. In my eyes you are the most wonderful kind of Japanese."

He hung up and I burst into tears. When, I wondered, would this awful nightmare of terror be over?

At ten in the morning on the next day the German and Japanese staff of the embassy gathered in the rotunda. Shafts of light shone down from the circle of windows high above the marble pillars. It reminded me of a picture in a book my father showed me when I was a little girl. It was a picture of a church in Rome. "Our Norwegian churches are darker," he had said. "We are obliged to find the light within ourselves. The peoples of southern Europe bring the light into their lives from the outside. But if you do not have the light burning inside you, there will be no light anywhere."

Ambassador Stahmer came down the staircase dressed in military uniform with his Iron Cross, received for bravery in battle in World War I, over his heart. He cleared his throat.

"Thank you all for assembling today," he said. "One or two have been detained, otherwise everyone is here, I believe. I will not keep you long. I simply wish to inform you that the fires caused by the cowardly American bombing of Tokyo have all nearly been put out and order has returned to the city. Our Japanese allies are unwavering in their knowledge that the Japanese people will fight on until the enemy is destroyed. As for the Fatherland ..."

He went on to give a highly censored version of events occurring in Germany and neighbouring countries, finishing with "the Thousand-Year Reich will soon be celebrating a glorious victory. Heil Hitler!" The staff members rose to their feet, saluted the ambassador and repeated his call. Inomata-san and I also rose to our feet, but we did not salute or move our lips. Donald Meissner, standing directly behind me, tapped me on the shoulder. I turned around. He handed me a folded piece of paper and indicated with his forefinger that I should go upstairs and read it in private. He smiled at me with parted lips as he tapped me on the shoulder again.

I unfolded the piece of paper at my desk. On it were these words …

Stanczuk is in Sugamo Prison. Ask to see Director Motomura when you get there and mention my name to him. Good luck!

Why was he encouraging me to seek Martin out? Was this part of a plan to get me arrested too? I confessed everything to Inomata-san, but he stopped me halfway through.

"Excuse me for interrupting, Bang-san, but I am aware of all of this. I know why Donald Meissner turned Martin-san in. He wanted those papers himself so that when the Americans come he can use them to barter for his freedom and save his own skin, tell them that he was sabotaging work at the embassy all the time. If Martin was around, his story might be challenged by him. He needed him out of the way. He knows, too, that you and Martin are planning to escape to Lake Nojiri. This morning he came right up to me, put his arm over my shoulder and said, 'Make sure you have enough petrol in the tank to get to the mountains and back. If not, I can always spare you some. Just let me know what you need.' He knows everything, that man."

"He knows."

"Yes. He's known all along. But he wants Martin and you out of the way now. You would only stand in his way. He is seeing into the future, that man, far into the future. All of the others here are too bound by the present, by surviving each day as it comes. Donald Meissner knows what he wants and he will get it. He won't let anyone stop him from clearing a path for his survival."

He did not show up at the nursing home that day. Perhaps he had gone to the hospital to visit his daughter. Or perhaps he himself was ill. I felt the need to see him. I was nervous all day long. I dropped a tray with a teapot and cups. The strength in my wrists and fingers had simply fallen away. The teapot shattered and I burned my bare right foot in its sandal with scalding tea. I also left an old woman in the toilet when I answered the phone in the corridor and forgot that she was there. She was only let out because Nurse Victoria passed by and heard her knocking on the inside. Was I too, like Margaret Miles, losing my memory? Was I, like her, losing sight of who I was?

That afternoon I went to the old Roseville Cinema on the Pacific Highway across from the station. I wanted to escape, if only for a few hours, from that nursing home and my own obsessions, to forget something I had not been able to forget for even a moment—myself. Unfortunately the film playing was *One Flew Over the Cuckoo's Nest* with its story set in a mental asylum. I didn't know whether to laugh at myself or cry. "Who knows, Liv Bang," I said to myself, "you might find yourself in just such a place one day." When I left the cinema a wave of heat struck my face and I was blinded by the light. It was so bright that even the air was hurting. The cars racing up and down the highway looked like blurred images on a screen, a moving mirage. The pavement undulated. The traffic noise was muffled. I must have stood by the signal for several minutes while it turned green and red and green again. I felt unable to move forward or backward from where I was, frozen in the bare heat of the day.

The next day, Tuesday, it was eleven-forty when he came into the home again. He was dressed in a blue blazer, tan trousers and beige sandshoes. Around his neck was a cravat decorated in a paisley pattern. A solid light-blue silk handkerchief, folded neatly into a pyramid, stuck out of the blazer's pocket. On his head was an ash-colour Panama hat. The residents of the Nola Road Nursing home had come to call him "Dapper Dan."

I had just emerged from the kitchen with a tray of sandwiches as he was walking with his stick up to his wife. He pulled a chair over to her with one hand and sat down beside her. He took her hand in his and began to talk to her. As I walked by I could hear that he was speaking German.

I avoided going near them as I served lunch to the residents, taking each one's tray to his chair and placing it on the little table in front of him.

"Victoria, would you take Mrs. Miles's tray to her please?"

"Sure, Liv. Give it here. Is there a drink for Mr. Miles too?"

"No, sorry."

"No worries. I'll get one," she said, carrying the tray back into the kitchen.

After lunch I washed and stacked the dishes. I stood in the corridor observing him through the panes in the French doors. He seemed to be singing to her, swinging his forefinger as if it were a baton. She was staring up at the ceiling with her mouth open. She appeared to be asleep. Then he stood up, gripped the chair with one hand and put it back under the window. He wiped his brow with his handkerchief, lifting the brim of his hat, then carefully folded the handkerchief into its pyramid shape and eased it into his pocket.

I decided that it was time for me to speak to him. I had waited long enough. I told Victoria that I was leaving for a doctor's appointment and probably wouldn't be back. By the time I had picked up my handbag from the staff room he was nearly at the corner of Nola Road and Maclaurin Parade. I quickened my pace and caught up with him near the bottom of the slope.

"Oh, Mr. Miles."

He turned around and bowed his head, touching the brim of his hat.

"Do you mind if I walk with you? I'm just leaving too."

"Not at all. A pleasure. Though it will probably do your legs no good to walk at the pace of such an old man."

We took a few steps together up the steepest part of the slope.

"I do love this little street," he said, "particularly the crepe myrtle trees. We didn't have these in Europe. They won't flower for a good month from now, but when they do they have the most subtle and delicate colours, hard to describe really, pink, purple and every shade in between. They were classified by a Swede, you know, a man, his name escapes me, who introduced the plant to Linnaeus."

"I didn't know that."

In fact, I hadn't known the English name of this tree that in Japan we called *saru-suberi*, or monkey slide, because its trunk is so smooth a monkey can slide down it.

"Well, I am a fountain of useless information. You are Norwegian, are you not?"

Of course he knew that. How could he forget his little Norwegian princess!

"Yes. How do you know?"

"Oh, the accent. I knew a few Norwegians in Switzerland, some of whom collaborated and then realized their mistake and others who fought in the resistance and escaped. Both sides ended up in neutral Switzerland. Switzerland played its cards with both sides, you know. Sensible, wouldn't you say?"

"Are you from Switzerland?"

He stopped walking and, lowering his head, peered into my eyes.

"Yes. I am."

Then he took a step forward, gazing up at the leaves of the crepe myrtle trees on the nature strip.

"Do you recognize me?" I asked, not daring to look at him.

"Of course I do. You look after my wife, Margaret. And

I also saw you in the train. You retrieved my stick from the floor."

We came to the park that faced the Pacific Highway. The grass was covered in little wooden crosses, each with its own red paper poppy and ribbon attached, fluttering in the breeze.

"I arrived a bit late this morning because of the service."

"Service?"

"Yes," he said, taking off his hat. "It's Remembrance Day, the 11th of November, the date that marks the end of the war, World War I, that is. I lingered here at eleven on my way to see Margaret. It was very moving … the old Australian men … travelling so far away from home to fight and kill other men…. And the monument with the words 'Lest We Forget.'"

Once again he stopped in his tracks. I could see a tear rolling down his cheek. Could this be the same Donald Meissner, a man who never showed a single spark of empathy for anyone, a man who thought only of his own skin and the heart of his dear Fatherland? Could I have been mistaken all this time? Had my obsessiveness led me up a blind alley? For all I knew the real Donald Meissner had died in the years following the war. No. I would never forget that look in his eye, the look he gave me in the room on the second floor of the embassy when he called me by my first name, the look he gave me moments earlier under the branches of the crepe myrtle tree … the very same look … the very same eyes!

"Do you mind if I rest for a while in the park?" he asked. "I'm feeling out of breath. Not as young as I used to be."

"No. I don't mind. Sit down."

He walked to a bench with some difficulty and dropped down onto it, releasing his stick.

"Oh, you see, I'm dropping my stick every time I am with you."

I sat beside him, picked up the stick and laid it across my lap.

The fresh green leaves of the large maple tree hanging over stone monument were trembling, and galahs were foraging for food among the crosses.

"Have you read the names on that monument?" he asked. "By the way, I haven't asked your name."

"Liv. Liv Bang."

I used my old name on purpose, pronouncing it emphatically while looking straight into his blue eyes. It was a name he would have been familiar with.

"Miss Bang," he said, not flinching in the least, "have you taken a look at the names engraved into the stone?"

"No. I am always in a hurry when I pass by this park."

"They are the names of local boys who went into battle. Some families are represented by more than one name. There is one name, Strange, that has four of those sent off to the last war. Imagine, four boys or men from one local family! And it happened only a generation or two ago and yet no one really cares except those few relatives who either remember the men or were told their stories. Just stories, Miss Bang. Tragic. Awful. Unimaginable. But now nothing more than stories."

He removed his hat and smoothed down his white hair with his handkerchief.

"Were you in the last war yourself, Mr. Miles?"

"Me?" he said, folding the handkerchief and placing it carefully in his breast pocket. "No. No. I wasn't. No. Being Swiss, we were spared all that. But I had an uncle in Germany. He had fought in the first war, received the Iron Cross, and then volunteered for the second one, though he was fifty when the war broke out and had no skills they needed. He was a floor manager at the KaDeWe Department Store in Berlin. I visited him there once in the mid-1920s. He was living an idyllic life, despite the inflation. But it all came to an end before long. He did enlist and ended up taking charge of supply lines to the Eastern front. He made himself useful after all. Sorry, I don't know why I'm going on and on like this. Must be something I sensed in a fellow European. The French have a word for it. 'Rapport.' I feel a rapport with you, perhaps because you are a European also transplanted down here."

"Transplanted? I never thought of it that way."

He turned his gaze from me to the grass in front of us.

"See these crosses? The Aussies here call the grass in this park on this day 'the field of crosses.' The tragedy of Europe brought home to Australia in the shape of a little wooden cross sunk into the parched grass once a year. It doesn't bear thinking about."

I searched his face for features similar to those on the face of *that man*. Donald Meissner had had a narrow nose with small nostrils, thin pencil lips and ears that stuck out on an angle from his scalp. Daniel Miles's features were different ... and yet the eyes were the same exact colour with the same exact look, and the voice, though weaker and mellower, had the same rasp when making a point about something. I knew in my bones that this was the same man.

"I knew a Bang, you know," he finally said.

"A young woman?"

"Oh no. I wish. An oldish man, I'm afraid."

"It's not an uncommon name in Norway."

"He had been fighting the Nazis in northern Norway, moving from place to place on skis. The Nazis captured his group and tortured them, but he managed to slip away in a blizzard. He made his way to Sweden and then eventually to Switzerland, remaining there for the duration of the war. After the war he went home to Norway. When he came back to Switzerland for a visit in 1949 he was already a wealthy man. Made his money in shipping, from Norway to Germany of all places. He took me for a spin in the fancy American car he had driven all the way from Oslo, a black Studebaker. Then, when we were out in the countryside, all of a sudden he stepped down on the accelerator pedal. We started to go forward at great speed. 'Truls,' I said, 'slow down.' But he gritted his teeth and kept going faster and faster and, it being Switzerland, there aren't many straight roads, I can tell you that. I looked at him. He was off somewhere in northern Norway, fleeing the Germans, skiing down a slope or something at breakneck speed. 'Truls,' I shouted, 'for God's sake, stop!' Luckily this brought him to his senses and he slowed down just before we hit a hairpin turn. I've never been so scared in my entire life. With some people the war simply continues on inside them. So it was with my Norwegian friend. Do you miss Norway, Miss Bang?"

"I've hardly been there. I spent my youth in Japan."

"Japan? Really?"

Again he looked at me without blinking an eye.

"I went to the United States shortly after the war," he said. "Met a number of Norwegians there too, though I was in Los Angeles and most of them were up in Minnesota and places. You would have thought they had had enough of the cold. Being away from your home country makes people nostalgic for everything they once knew there, even terrible things like the freezing cold and long winter nights. One thing about nostalgia for one's country: It gets more intense and passionate the longer one stays away from it. One's country, with all its awful traditions and oppressive customs, looks better and better as the years go by. The brain is the body's most sentimental organ, not the heart, Miss Bang. The heart just retains all the slights, blows and scars of the past. They never leave its chambers. The brain turns the old canvas, painted in thick dark oils, into a serene pastel landscape and just folds it away.

"No nostalgia for me, though, Miss Bang. I haven't lived in my country for decades now. Would never go back. Wouldn't even go back to America. The people there are very nice, but you must recognize their country as heaven on Earth for them to accept you. They think they are the mouthpiece of God. When an individual begins acting like God you should be wary. When a whole country does so you should be terrified. No, I like Australia. Everyone here faces forward, shoulder to shoulder, as they march quietly together into the future. I love the Australian sun. It shines so brightly that it even obliterates shadows."

"You wouldn't go back to your country, you said? Did you mean Germany?"

He put his hat on, took the stick from my lap and, using it as a crutch, stood up.

"You haven't been listening to a thing I've said, have you."

"Not at all. I meant to say Switzer…."

"Never mind," he said, stepping across the grass and weaving his way among the crosses, then turning back to me. "I'm just a boring old man. No stories to tell that a beautiful woman would bother listening to."

I watched him reach the highway and walk towards the traffic signal. The traffic came to a halt. He crossed the highway and went down the stairs to the platform at Roseville Station. I stood by the bench for some time. From where I was I could not read the names engraved into the monument. They all formed a single grey block framed in stone under the now still maple tree.

That night I phoned Karen.

"Oh Liv, good to hear from you. I couldn't make it to see grandma. Sorry! Had a date, actually. Stan. Did I mention him to you? We're kind of a thing."

"Congratulations."

"Congratulate me in a fortnight if we still are."

"Look, I'm going into the city tomorrow and thought you might be able to meet, say, at two? For coffee?"

"That'd be great. I'm finished with course work and everything. That's it. I'm outta uni. A free bird. Whoopee!"

"Well, we'll have to celebrate. I can't make lunch but I know a great place with amazing cakes and coffee."

"I'm yours. Where is it?"

"It's on Elizabeth St. The Hellenic Club."

"Don't you have to be a member to go to clubs like that?"

"Not this one. You don't even have to be Greek."

"Ace. I'll look it up in the white pages. I'll see you there."

I would only have about five and a half hours before then to find out the information that I needed. I had two things to go on, two little pieces of information that would link the kindly dapper gentleman with the neatly folded handkerchief to the beast I knew him to be.

The next day I arrived at the State Library of New South Wales on Macquarie St. when it opened at nine. It was only a short walk from there to the Hellenic Club. I packed a sandwich and an apple so that I wouldn't have to leave the library for lunch. I went directly to the reference desk.

"I wonder if you would be able to help me," I said to the woman behind the desk. She was in her late fifties or early sixties, but was wearing faded jeans and a tie-dyed Indian blouse.

"What would you like?"

"Do you have a list of people, Germans, I mean, who were awarded the Iron Cross in World War I?"

"Germans with an Iron Cross?"

"Yes. Look, I know it's not the usual sort of question."

"No, that's okay. Well, as a matter of fact, you are in luck, in a way. I used to be an historian of European history up at the University of Queensland."

"Oh, then I am truly fortunate."

"In one way, yes. In another, no."

"What do you mean?"

"Do you know how many Germans were awarded an Iron Cross, if you include all three classes?"

"No."

"Hundreds of thousands. Probably millions, in fact. I'm not even sure the Germans themselves have a list or know how many of them were given out. Are you looking for a particular person who received one?"

"Yes I am, actually."

"Famous?"

"Pardon?"

"Was this man famous?"

"No, I don't think so. He worked in a department store. I know his last name."

"It doesn't matter where he worked. With no real list extant, I'm afraid you've got Buckleys of finding out what you're after."

"Buckleys?"

"Yeah, no chance at all. Wouldn't know where to start."

It was just ten minutes past nine and my first lead had already vanished into thin air.

"Did you say department store?" she asked, putting a bobby pin between her teeth, separating its prongs and sliding it into her dyed brown hair.

"Yes. In Berlin."

"What was its name?"

"The store's name?"

"Yes."

"Um, let's see. I wrote it down last night. It's, here it is, it's the KaDeWe Department Store. It's in Berlin, or was in Berlin at one time."

"My German isn't very good, but it sounds like the initials of something. Can you wait for a while?"

"Oh yes, I have all morning. Just the morning, though."

I stood in the middle of the spacious reading room where about a dozen people, most of them my age or older, were already seated at tables, reading or writing. I hadn't prepared myself for waiting and had brought nothing to read. I went to a nearby shelf with reference works on it, removed a book titled *Chinese Temples of Old Victoria* and carried it to a table. Within minutes, however, the librarian had come from the stacks toting six or seven volumes.

"These may be of some help," she said, placing them in a pile on the table. "Apparently the department store is very famous, though I must admit I hadn't heard of it. I've never been to Berlin, east or west. The KaDeWe stands for Kaufhaus des Westens. It's apparently where your posh people shop in Berlin. Guess it must be in the west."

I thanked her and began leafing through the books, which were all photographic directories of buildings in Berlin before the war. All of the books were in German. Despite the passage of years I could still read the language with some ease. I was careful not to miss a page. It was past eleven when I finished going through the books. There was one photo of the façade of the KaDeWe Department Store in the 1930s, but none taken on the inside.

I took the books back to the reference desk.

"I'm sorry but I found nothing."

"I see. That's too bad. Look, can you leave it with me for a day or two? Let me know exactly what …"

"No!" This word, coming out in a loud voice, seemed to shock her. "I'm sorry. You see, I need the information today. I must leave here before two."

"All right, if that's the case," she said, jerking her head back and blinking her eyes. "I'll give it another try. Why don't you go out and have lunch or something."

"Yes. I'll be back in fifteen minutes."

"Fifteen minutes? I'm not superhuman, you know."

"I'm sorry."

"Okay. What is it I am supposed to be looking for?"

"Any photographs of the inside of the department store or of the people who worked there."

"Got it. You go have lunch now."

She turned away and walked towards the door that led to the stacks.

I sat on the library steps eating my sandwich and apple as I observed the people walking by. It was a cooler morning than on the previous days. It had been a long time since I had been in the city at this time of day. I wrapped the apple core in the Glad Wrap from the sandwich and went back into the building. The person I had talked to was not behind the desk. Instead there was a lanky young man with a bushy head of hair and stubble on his chin resembling an outgrowth of moss. He was in conversation with a woman who looked Japanese.

"Excuse me, is the lady who was here before …"

"I beg your pardon, I'm serving someone here. I'll thank you to please wait," he scowled, turning back to the woman and saying some words in such heavily accented Japanese it was clear she could not understand him. She cocked her head to one side. It was obvious that it was no use pursuing her query, so she bowed, saying "*Arigato gozaimasu* (Thank you very much)," and walked out of the library.

"Gail'll be back at one," he said, throwing his head back and rushing past me towards the door to the stacks.

I sat down and waited for over an hour. I was so agitated that I couldn't read or think straight. At one I saw Gail return from lunch.

"Hello," I called, running up to her. "Did you find something?"

"Let me at least put my bag down."

"But my time is running out."

"Geezus, give a girl a minute, will ya?"

She placed her handbag on her chair, adjusted two bobby pins in her hair and leaned over the reference desk.

"Okay, now. As a matter of fact I did find one book. Here it is. It's a kind of celebration of thirty years, an anniversary of the opening of the store in 1907. It has lots of photos. I'm afraid this is all we've got on the subject. If what you're looking for isn't here, I don't think you'll find it anywhere in Australia."

"Oh thank you," I said, grabbing the book from her and rushing to the table.

The book was full of photographs of all of the floors of the KaDeWe Department Store. There were stylish shoppers enjoying lunch in the opulent checkered-floor food court, with murals over the archway depicting the harvesting and production of food; and groups of well-to-do Berliners standing by well-stocked glass-top counters. At the very back of the book was a photograph of the staff, taken in 1931. The faces were very small, as were the names below. I went back to the reference desk.

"Excuse me, may I borrow a magnifying glass?"

The woman named Gail, speaking on the telephone, reached into the top drawer of her desk, produced a large magnifying glass and plopped it down without interrupting her conversation.

"Thank you," I whispered.

She nodded her head and continued to speak on the phone.

I held the magnifying glass above the photograph and stared into it. There must have been a hundred or more employees in it, standing in eight or nine rows. The people in the front row were seated. The title at the top of the page read, in German, "Managerial and Sales Staff." I scanned the names. And there it was, precisely what I was looking for. Listed as seated in the front row, fifth from the left was the name I needed: Werner Meissner.

That's it! That's his uncle … or his father! He was lying all along. He himself lived in Berlin. His uncle or father, Werner, was a floor manager at the KaDeWe Department Store. It all made perfect sense—the name, the location, the social status of a man whose nephew or son was to become an officer in the SS. He had lied to me about being Swiss. But why had he gone so far as to alter the features of his face? It was clear to me. After the war many people doctored documents to hide real names, doctored features with surgery to hide real faces, doctored the past itself to pretend that it had never existed. Well, it had existed, Donald Meissner. You had existed. You may change the trappings of your appearance and the nature of your "story." But you cannot change the wicked things you did to people. Those people will not change their story to suit your "new" life. They will not forget the man you were … and *are.*

The next morning Donald Meissner had arranged for an embassy car, a black 770 model Daimler-Benz, to take me to Sugamo Prison.

"This car will take you to your dear little man," he said, opening the car door for me. "You know, Fräulein Bang, we have managed to pass over the dog and we will make it over the tail too."

"What is that supposed to mean?"

"Oh sorry. It's an old German proverb. It means that this will all soon come to an end."

"This?" I said, staring at him through the half-open window of the car. "What is *this*?"

He nodded his head over and over again, saying, "Yes. This. The rabid dog of war will very soon escape our clutches, no doubt straight into the clutches of others in some other country. The trick is to make sure you yourself have not been bitten and that the dog never again shows up at your doorstep."

The drive took about thirty minutes. There were very few cars on the road. The fires set by the bombing had been extinguished; but, in any case, they had occurred across the river, in the opposite direction of the prison.

When I arrived at the prison, I was met by a man in a brown three-piece suit and check necktie. He was flanked by two uniformed guards.

"Welcome, Miss Bang," he said in lightly accented English. "I have been told about you. I am Director Motomura. It is a pleasure to host you."

He led me through the gates and into the building. We came out onto a dirt courtyard where a small group of soldiers were marching with rifles held in front of them. We turned a corner and passed a massive iron door with the number 13 written in white on it. I knew this to be the entrance to the execution room because the staircase leading up to the hangman's noose was called the *jusan kaidan*, the "staircase with thirteen steps."

"He is being held in here," said the director, opening another metal door and putting out his right palm to indicate that I should go through. He entered after me, followed by the two guards. We walked down a corridor of cells with a raised barred grill running down the middle of the floor. The guards, in the lead by then, halted, stomped their feet twice and unbolted the door.

"Please," said the director, once again thrusting out his open palm. "Do not take more than fifteen minutes, Miss Bang. It is unprecedented that we allow such a visit at all. It is thanks to Mr. Meissner. You are deeply in his debt for this."

Director Motomura retreated, and the door was slammed shut.

Martin was sitting on a small wooden chair in the corner. He was hunched over and did not immediately acknowledge my presence. Without saying a word I went up to him, fell to my knees and brought his hands to my lips. His torso and head began to shake. He was sobbing uncontrollably.

"My darling, my love," I said. "It's me. Liv. I am your life, remember? … Your Liv. Shh. Shh. Please don't cry."

His body continued to shake and rock from side to side. He

would still not show his face to me.

"It's all right, my love," I said, holding back my own tears as best as I could. "You will be out of here soon. I promise you. The bombing has stopped for now. But it is bound to start up again all over the city. We will get away, just the two of us. I promise you that. Inomata-san will drive us in his car. He's ready to do it the day you come out. We'll go to the lake. You will be your old self again."

His head stopped moving, and gradually his body became still.

"My darling," I said, kissing his hands. "My dearest."

He lifted up his head to look at me. His entire face had been bashed in. He could only open one eye, and even then just barely. The flesh around both his eyes was swollen and puffed. Caked blood formed a rivulet running from his right temple down his cheek and neck, disappearing under the open collar of his shirt. His right ear was so covered in dry blood that it looked like a plum. He parted his lips in a smile and I could see that he had no front upper teeth.

"Oh my God, what have they done to you?"

I put my arms around him and began to weep.

"Now, sugar snail, you stop crying," he whispered in a voice that I could barely hear.

"Martin … I can't … I can't …"

"Shh, my darling. It's all right. My sweet little mouse."

"But you … that man sent you to be …"

"No. It wasn't just him. It is the war itself. I am paying for my country's sins. All Germans, both good and bad, must share blame. That way the burden on each one of us will be more bearable. But listen. They found no incriminating papers on me and are bound to let me go soon. They've done much worse to people in these cells. I'm a lucky one. And I have you. My Liv, my life."

Martin was embracing me tightly. We remained like that in

the corner for some minutes without speaking to each other. I realized that we wouldn't have more than five minutes left.

"Now you listen," I said, standing. "I am going to save my tears for later, so they can be tears of joy. Darling, listen. Tell them whatever you need to. It hardly matters now. They haven't executed any foreigners here since they hanged Sorge last year, and he was much more of a threat to them than you will ever be. I will come back to get you. Leave it to me. I am going to get you freed very soon."

"How are you going to do that?" he said, rising with great effort by bracing himself against the wall.

"I will do it. It simply requires a word from Donald Meissner."

"I will not allow *that man* to play a part in my freedom!" cried Martin, banging his left fist on the wall. "They plunged my head in water and held me down. I couldn't breathe … I can't let …"

"Shh, calm down, my love. It doesn't matter now how you attain your freedom, all we have to do is …"

"Yes it does. Yes it does!"

"Listen to me. Martin, calm down! We don't have much time. This is no time for demanding truth or for insisting on justice. There will be time for that later. The Americans will firebomb this city into oblivion, this prison along with it. The guards and everyone will run away. Do you want to burn alive locked in your cell? We can be away from here. We can live together, just the two of us. And when this war is over we can go wherever we like. All you have to do is leave Donald Meissner alone. Do not try to get your papers back from him. Let them be his. Let him do what he wishes with them."

"How can I do that? He is a man who has spent his life sending innocent people to torture chambers and to their graves. Now he wants to use the papers to bargain for his own freedom."

"Yes, he has many victims, and I don't want you to be his last."

The cell door opened.

"Liv, Liv. I love you so much."

"I know, my darling. I love you. I love you with my life. We have one life now. That's why you must do as I say."

We stared at each other, our eyes welling with tears. I turned about and walked out of the cell. Martin was standing erect with his back flush against the wall. Both fists were clenched at his sides.

Things moved quickly after that. Donald Meissner informed Director of Sugamo Prison Motomura that Martin was to be released and returned to the embassy. Two days later, in the early evening, he arrived. He walked slowly with a stick. He wore a pair of dark glasses that he was given at the prison. He was able to see out of one eye. His right ear was entirely covered in a gauze patch held in place by shiny black tape. Without entering the building he was transferred to the same car that had taken me to the prison, and the two of us returned home.

After two weeks of rest Martin's appearance was nearly back to normal. I removed the gauze patch on his ear. The ear itself was intact but he could not hear with it. He had been running a low fever since coming home and was struck by dizzy spells several times a day. Once he fainted in the bath. Luckily I was with him, soaping myself, and immediately pulled his head out of the water.

It was the end of April by the time we felt that he was well enough to travel to Lake Nojiri. I was still going every day to the embassy, fulfilling my duties as a translator of foreign broadcasts together with Inomata-san, who was not as skillful as Martin when it came to operating the radio. The Americans had landed on the islands of Okinawa, including the main island itself, and fierce battles were raging, battles being won by the Americans according to what we heard on our radio and by the Japanese if you believed the announcements on Japanese radio. President Roosevelt had passed away and Vice President Truman had become president. In Europe British troops had liberated a concentration camp in northern Germany, finding tens of thousands of prisoners on the verge of death.

Donald Meissner was still arriving at the embassy in his immaculately starched uniform. He seemed to take an inordinate pride in his appearance. Ambassador Stahmer wore the same crumpled suit every day. He had apparently sent his uniform and his Iron Cross back to Germany "for safe keeping." The Japanese staff at the embassy had been dismissed and urged to return to their hometowns. Tokyo had become unsafe, though the firebombing of Osaka, Nagoya and almost every other big and small city was just as thorough and unforgiving. Inomata-san and the chauffeur of the embassy's Daimler-Benz, old Baba-san, were the only Japanese staff remaining. The Germans had stayed put. As one of them, a young pretty secretary named Rosemarie, whose home was in Hamburg, said to me, "I am probably less likely to lose my life here than at home."

When the day of our departure arrived we waited on the street outside the only home we had ever lived in together. All we were taking to Lake Nojiri was the two suitcases at our feet. Passersby either took no notice of us or stared at us with incredulity, as if we had come from another planet to which we were about to return. One old man, Numata-san, a neighbour, rushed out of his door with a large *furoshiki* cloth, handed the bundle to us, bowed deeply, turned about and scurried back into his house without so much as a word.

The black Daimler-Benz pulled up in front of the lodging house. Baba-san jumped out, tripping over a rock in the middle of the road but managing to stay on his feet, and trotted around the boot of the car, opening the back-seat door for us. He picked up our suitcases, unlocked the boot and placed them neatly in it, then returned to the back-seat door and gently closed it, tipping his cap.

"Baba-san," I said. "I thought that we were going to travel to Nagano in Inomata-san's car?"

"Ah yes," he said, sitting in the driver's seat and turning his head halfway around. "But Mr. Meissner decided that Inomata-san was needed in the embassy to inform him on what is happening in Japan and the world. With you and Stanczuk-san gone, the room would be empty without him. He is now so important, more important than Ambassador Stahmer, I think."

Driving out of the city of Tokyo that morning I felt a great burden being lifted off my shoulders. Martin and I were not exactly free. We were still prisoners of the war, and we would not find our freedom until it was over. But we were no longer employees of the German embassy. And we were out of the reach of the one man there who had once held our fate in his hands.

I managed to get to the Hellenic Club a few minutes before two. I climbed the stairs to the restaurant and told the head waiter that one other person was coming, asking for a table by the window overlooking Hyde Park.

"Certainly, madam," he said, throwing a white tea towel over his forearm and smiling broadly. "This is our not busy time. All tables free for you."

A large group of people had gathered on a grass clearing in the park across the street. They were being addressed by a long-haired man dressed in blue jeans, a striped shirt and purple necktie. A few of the people held placards …

Kerr's Cur

Khemlani Votes Liberal

We Want Gough!

"They don't like what happened," said the waiter, plonking two glasses of ice water on the white tablecloth. "In Greece, generals come and shove people around, punch, arrest and torture. Here democracy. It is Greek word but no longer in our vocabulary. Here good democracy. People can protest."

Just then Karen appeared, followed by a young man with a trim beard.

"Hi," she said, walking up to me. "This is Stan. I hope it's okay that I brought him. We're kind of inseparable now. Jooles has done a runner. Didn't pay her portion of the bloody rent either."

"Of course it's okay," I said, standing. "Hello, Stan, nice to meet you. I'm Liv."

"Karen's told me about you."

"Liv, Stan's been to Denmark. I know it's not Norway, but it's kind of alike, isn't it?"

"Absolutely. We Scandinavians are all part of the same family. We also understand each other's languages, except that we say that Danes speak with hot potatoes in their throat."

"Yeah," said Stan, "whenever they spoke it sounded like they were drowning."

We all laughed. The waiter came by and put another glass of water on the table. I ordered three Greek coffees.

"Stan's been OS, so he's …"

"OS?"

"Yeah, overseas."

"Oh, I see."

"… so he's going to take me first to the places he knows

really well, like Turkey and Yugoslavia, which is supposed to be unbelievably cheap. Hey, Stan, what's the place named after the dogs?"

"The Dalmatian Coast?"

"Yeah, that's it. We don't have much money but we can get jobs, can't we, I mean in Europe?"

"Easy as pie," said Stan, drinking half a glass of water in one long gulp. "Aussies are really loved everywhere you go. We're like Americans only without the baggage. Know what I mean, Liv?"

He glanced out the window. The man in the purple necktie was still speaking to the protesters.

"Oh, there's a demonstration on, Karen," said Stan. "Let's join it after. Look, someone's even got a placard about Khemlani. He's the shady businessman backed by the reactionaries to get Whitlam out of power. The bloody shits. It's a coup, that's what it is. They killed off everything we fought for. Only in Australia would the reactionaries call themselves 'the Liberals.' And now we're going straight back to good old white philistine Australia. I'm not coming back, Karen. Never. This country is one big pisshole."

Prime Minister Gough Whitlam had been dismissed from office by Governor-General John Kerr on Remembrance Day, the very day that "Daniel Miles" and I had spoken in the park at Roseville. I had not been interested in Australian politics until Gough Whitlam had become leader and had turned the country into a welfare state like Germany and Norway.

The waiter arrived carrying a large tray. On it was not only three coffees, served in small cups, but three portions of cake.

"This is *samali*," he said. "It is traditional Greek cake. Very nice. Smells of rosewater and lemon. That is the smell of my country, roses and lemons. Don't you worry. There is no charges. It is on my house."

"Thank you very much," I said, putting portions in front of

Karen and Stan, who were sitting opposite me. "There's what looks like pine nuts embedded in it. I haven't had those for years."

The waiter, standing above us, smiled a big toothy smile, threw his arms into the air in a gesture of joy and returned to the bar, above which was a long polished mirror and a row of Greek wine bottles.

"Stan's a rebel, Liv," said Karen, taking a dessert fork from the tray.

"That's good. We need rebels in this world."

"He spent three months in Nepal and became a Buddhist. His mother followed him there, right into the temple, and tried to bribe him. She had this JAP all lined up for him and ..."

"Jap? You mean, Japanese?"

"No. JAP. Jewish Australian Princess. His parents were more worried about him marrying some shiksa ... isn't that what you call them, Stan? ... than they were about him scuttling the religion. The Rosens are atheist Jews anyway. They wouldn't be caught dead in a synagogue. His dad smokes his own bacon."

"Mum kept upping the ante. Ten thousand, thirty thousand. A new car of my choice. Anything to get me back to Bellevue Hill—it's, like, crawling with Jews there and they're all filthy rich—and into the clutches of one of her girlfriend's daughters."

"So, he's got me instead. I'm not Jewish or rich. But I have nothing against shacking up with a Buddhist atheist rebel, especially one like Stan."

The crowd in the park across the street was dispersing.

"So, Liv," said Karen, "what brings you into the city?"

"Oh, I was just doing some research."

"Research? Are you writing something, a book or something?"

"No, not exactly. Just looking into things."

"Liv's an expert on Italian art, Stan."

"Oh no I'm not. I just ... look, Karen, while you're here I just wanted to mention something to you."

"Yeah, sure. I read that book you gave me. Stan's reading it now."

"That's wonderful. This is something, actually, about your grandfather."

"Grandpa Dan? Did you meet him at the nursing home or something? Stan, Liv's volunteering at the nursing home where my grandma's living. Grandma's kind of, well, not all there."

"She has senile dementia," I said. "She has lost her memory and doesn't recognize the people she once knew."

"It must be really hard on your grandpa, Karen."

"Yeah. But he's strong," she said.

"Yes, it must be hard on him," I said. "Anyway, listen. While I was just doing some research, I mean, about something else, you know, I came across something in an old book … and, well, um, actually, it concerns your grandfather."

"My grandfather in a book?"

"Well, not your grandfather himself but a relative of his, with the same name, an uncle, or perhaps his own father."

"Far out."

"Yes. Well, the riddle of it all, um, I mean, the thing that's still not all that clear is that your grandfather may not be Swiss at all."

"But he was Swiss. I saw his old passport."

"I don't know about that. But it appears that he may actually have been German."

"German? Well, he speaks German. But he was Swiss. He went to America and they gave him citizenship there, then he came here to Australia."

"Well, I just wanted you to know. Ask him about it. See what he says."

"German, eh?" said Stan, downing his coffee with a grimace. "Oh, that's so sweet. I prefer Italian espresso. So then, what did he do in the war? I vas jast followink orders!"

"There's no need to go into that," I said, taking a drink of water. "Look, it's probably nothing, some sort of coincidence. What's history without its coincidences, I mean. Without them you'd have to make them up in order to make things hang together."

"Shit, the demonstrators have gone," said Stan. "We're too late. Well, there's more where that came from. We are going to protest and protest until Gough is made prime minister again. Only Australians would allow this sort of thing to happen and not care. What a ratbag country this is."

We walked down the stairs to the street. There was a light rain falling.

"Where are you going from here, Karen?" I asked.

"Oh, back to Glebe. Stan's working on an article he wants to send to Nation Review. It's about how the Jews in Australia are so complacent. All they do is pretend nothing is ever wrong and live out their lives in quiet comfort. Is that right?"

"They're Australians," said Stan. "What do you expect?"

"Well, I don't expect much from any nationality really," I said. "We're pretty much all the same when it comes to doing nothing if we think our actions will threaten our personal comfort."

"Thanks very much for the coffee, Liv," said Karen, slipping her arm around Stan's waist.

"It's lovely to see a young couple so fond of each other. It's, well ... just lovely."

They could obviously see the tears that were in my eyes.

"Does it remind you of something ... of someone?" asked Stan.

"Yes. It does. A long time ago now. Goodbye, you two. Take good care of each other. That's the main thing."

"Oh we will, Liv," said Karen, squeezing Stan's waist. "I can promise you that."

I walked through the drizzling rain to Town Hall Station

and took the train home.

She will definitely bring it up with him, I thought. I have planted a seed that will germinate, a seed that has been waiting in the soil for decades to see the light of day and bring forth *life*.

The three months that Martin and I spent together at Lake Nojiri were idyllic. I looked back at them in later years as the most beautiful time of my life. Not that the circumstances of daily life were in any way ideal. Primitive, that's the word for it. The hut, or shack, we occupied had only a single room, which functioned as living room, dining room, kitchen, bedroom and, behind a rough hemp string curtain, toilet that once flushed but now required hefty plunges and a bucket of well water to rid itself of the contents of its bowl. Food was scarce. The *furoshiki* that our neighbour Numata-san had given us contained plump sweet potatoes, a lidded earthenware tub of country-style miso, a medium-size bottle of soy sauce and a bundle of *naganegi*, or Japanese leeks. Our neighbours at the lake, almost all displaced foreigners like us, shared dried river fish, cabbage and unpolished rice with us, and some Japanese farmers in the district brought us eggs and, once, a whole chicken, despite the fact that it was dangerous for them to so much as associate with foreigners. We also had to endure unannounced visits by the Japanese police, who, after Germany's surrender in early May, considered German citizens enemy aliens.

One day in June we heard a car drive up and stop in front of our hut. It was late afternoon and we were just beginning to prepare a dinner made from the meagre leftovers of the day before. We exchanged glances. Martin tucked his shirt in his pants. He wanted to appear as respectable as possible when the local police called.

There was a knock at the door. I answered it. Much to our surprise it was not the police at all but Inomata-san. We hadn't heard from him since leaving the embassy.

"I am so sorry to come without warning you beforehand, Bang-san, Stanczuk-san," he said.

"Oh no, not at all," I said, hugging him, which was not something one usually did to a Japanese, not even a close friend or relative. I was that overjoyed to see him.

"I am on my way to my hometown in Fukui. It is not so much of a detour. At any rate, you know the expression *isogaba maware*."

"Yes. Martin, that means, 'When you are in a hurry, take the long way around.'"

"Sounds like the story of our life, Liv," said Martin. "The very long way around."

"You are so welcome, Inomata-san! Please sit down. You must be tired. How is Tokyo?"

We shared what little food we had for dinner. Inomata-san insisted on sleeping in his car. In any case there was nowhere for him to sleep in our little shack. This is what he told us ...

"Tokyo is utter chaos. The bombings have continued. People in the Japanese government want to surrender, but they feel they must have guarantees that the Emperor will not be removed from the throne and not be prosecuted for any reason whatsoever. The Army will not admit that it has lost the war, though many in the other branches of the military have already given up in their minds. As for the embassy, it too was bombed late last month and the building was destroyed. But no one was in it. Just after Germany's surrender, the Japanese police had raided the embassy and arrested everyone. I was not arrested because I am a Japanese, though if I remained in Tokyo I believe that I would be put behind bars. The staff, including Ambassador Stahmer and Herr Meissner, are being held in the old hotel in Miyanoshita, you know, up at Hakone.

They are being questioned, but I do not believe tortured or mistreated in any way. It is only a matter of days before the Americans claim victory in Okinawa. Then they will invade Honshu. Once they have taken Tokyo, the rest of the country will fall like a house built of matchsticks. You two have been lucky. You escaped the fire that is coming. You would have been arrested along with the ambassador and Herr Meissner. Perhaps Herr Meissner knew that something like that would happen and that is why he arranged for you both to leave before Germany's capitulation. I know that he is a man who has done many very bad things to people. Many people have died because of him, because he denounced them to the Japanese Kempeitai. But it is thanks to him that you have your freedom … and I have mine too. He gave me several containers of gasoline before I left, enough to get me back to Fukui. He knew that there was no gasoline left in Japan for private people. He may have had bad thoughts in his head, but he has some decency in his heart."

In the weeks after Inomata-san's visit Martin and I swam in the lake every day. We kept away from the other foreigners living by the lake. It wasn't out of a feeling of unfriendliness that we did this. All of us foreigners kept to ourselves at that time. We kept our fears to ourselves.

Only once did we all come together. It was on the night of August 15th, the day of the Japanese surrender. We too had listened to the Emperor's broadcast at noon in which he called upon his subjects to "endure the unendurable." Martin had fixed a broken radio and set it up on the lectern by the altar of a weatherboard church that had been built by missionaries in the late 19th century. All of us foreigners rejoiced, though it took a Portuguese priest who had lived seventy years in Japan to translate the speech for us. Even I had had trouble understanding it. But I did understand what the Emperor had meant when he mentioned the "unendurable." It was the humiliation of defeat. To us, however, the unendurable had come long before. From the day of Japan's surrender we were no longer enemies of the Japanese people.

Martin and I made love throughout that night. Perhaps it was the feeling of being unburdened by the iron weight of the war, or simply an expression of the hope that we both finally trusted. We would have a life together in a new place where we could forget the nightmares we had lived through.

"I love you so much, Liv," he said. "I once called you 'my life.' You are my life."

"And you will be mine, darling, forever. We'll start all over again as two new people."

"Yes ... now come here, little snail, and crawl on top of me."

But the ecstasy did not last long. A few days later the fever that had plagued Martin since being beaten in prison returned. He felt so weak that he could not get out of bed. Soon he was drifting in and out of consciousness. Luckily one of our neighbours at the lake was a physician, an Austrian Jew. The Japanese had not known what to do with him during the war, so they let him go to the lake and "disappear from view."

"He has meningitis, I fear," said Dr. Lipschitz. "He may have retained a grumbling infection in his ear that gradually worked its way into his brain."

"Is there any medicine for this? When will he get better?"

"The brain has membranes that protect it. But if the infection breaches those membranes, I am afraid that nothing can stop it from getting into his brain. There is no medicine here at all. But I do have some aspirin. Here, give two tablets to him four times a day. It will bring down the fever. I'm sorry but that is the best I can do for him."

The aspirin did reduce Martin's fever. But he fell into a coma, coming out of it only once. It was into that little window of his consciousness that I was able to bring him the news for the first time that I was pregnant. He stared into my eyes with tears streaming down his face. He was unable to speak. In the early hours of the next morning, Martin passed away. We buried him in a plot in the woods beside the lake with a cross made out of red pine branches as a marker. An old French pastor said a few kind words over his grave. After the funeral he took my elbow in his hand and led me to the shore of the lake.

"Martin must remain a symbol to you and all of us of what Germans can become in the future," said the pastor. "He will rest in peace here forever now."

I stayed on at Lake Nojiri until the beginning of November, simply going through the motions of life. When American soldiers came through that month they wrote down all our names and began to make arrangements for our evacuation, for some to Tokyo, for others back to their country of origin. I returned to Tokyo, three months later giving birth to a baby boy at a hospital staffed by American military doctors and nurses. He weighed only 1,800 grams but, thanks to being put in an incubator, survived. I named him Martin and kept him until the early summer of 1946 when I "went back" to Norway. There was no way that I could guarantee the welfare of my beautiful little boy. I was persuaded by the doctors and nurses at the hospital to give him up for adoption. I know that an officer in the occupation force and his wife adopted Martin, but I never found out their name. My son is no doubt living somewhere in the United States today. He would be turning thirty next year. I would like to say that not a day has gone by that I have not thought about him, but that would be untrue. Once I came to Australia I virtually forgot that I once had a son. But I never forgot his namesake, Martin, the most wonderful man I have ever known. He suffered so much because of where he was born. He had a passion for life and a faith in people's goodness that was not dampened by war. I loved him so much for what he stood for and I miss the passion that he had for me and what he saw in me. When he died, the person I was died with him.

I decided to leave well enough alone for the time being. Three weeks passed before I made contact with anyone from the Meissner family except Margaret. I continued to go to the Nola Road Nursing Home, making it a point to spend time with her. Her husband did not show up once during that time.

"It's very odd," said Mrs. Archibold, taking the cover off the cushion where Mr. Somerset, the man who had stripped and danced under the chandelier, had sat. He had died in his sleep the night before. "Mr. Miles was the most frequent visitor of all the relatives."

"Perhaps he's ill," I said, taking Margaret Miles's teacup from her. "Don't you want your tea, Margaret?"

"No," she scowled. "It's much too strong. Is it you who stole my lipstick? *Diebin*! (Thief!)"

"No. Oh dear, we'll have to look for it, Mrs. Miles," I said, taking her hands in mine. Then I turned to Mrs. Archibold. "Perhaps he's gone somewhere on vacation, with Christmas coming soon, visiting family in another city or overseas, I mean."

"Not likely. He has no other family."

"Do you know that?"

"Yes. He told me as much himself. 'Margaret, my daughter and my granddaughter are all the people I have in the world,' he said. Here, I'll take that."

I handed her the teacup. She walked towards the open French doors.

"Oh, Mrs. Archibold?"

She turned around.

"Yes?"

"I'll be leaving before two today. I've got a doctor's

appointment."

I had said this in a loud voice. Several of the residents turned their head in my direction.

"Nothing serious, I trust."

"Um, no no. Just routine."

She smiled and went through the doors towards the kitchen.

Actually my leaving early had nothing at all to do with my health. I had looked up Marlis Ditzen's number in the white pages the night before and phoned her. There was only one Ditzen in the telephone book—M Ditzen.

"It was very kind of you to visit me at the hospital," she had said on the phone.

"Not at all. Are you fully recovered from your operation?"

"Oh, uh, yes, thank you."

"Look, I know it's forward of me, but would you like to meet in the city sometime, say, tomorrow afternoon around three?"

"As it happens, I am going into the city to do some shopping," she said, "so, yes, that would be lovely. Where would you like to meet?"

"Well, how about Circular Quay? The Opera House steps? You know, it's been open for two years and I've never been there."

"You haven't?"

"No," I said. "I rarely get into the city. I work at home, and ..."

I heard the faint sound of a buzzer through the receiver.

"Oh sorry, someone's at the door. We're on. See you at three tomorrow. Bye, Liv."

I arrived at the Opera House steps fifteen minutes early and stood on the paving stones overlooking the harbour. Two ferries were passing each other between the Opera House and the bridge, and a few sailboats were gliding slowly over the still water. It was another sweltering day, and I could feel the heat rising in waves from the paving stones onto my arms and face. I walked around the building to the front steps. Marlis, wearing what I recognized to be a Marimekko floral print dress and wide-brim straw hat, waved to me.

"Sorry to be so abrupt on the phone last night," she said. "It was my father. He came for a rare visit. He hadn't been to my place for some time. By the way, how is mother? I really should be seeing her, but with the operation and everything...."

"She's fine. I mean, no change."

"Does she recognize you?"

"Well, not really. Every day I have to reintroduce myself and show her my badge, and every day she says 'So nice to meet you.' But I've taken to using a bit of German with her. She seems to respond to that."

"I would imagine so," she said as we walked away from the building and up the knoll past the spreading Moreton Bay fig trees. "Ah, I love these trees. I saw them for the first time when we arrived here twenty years ago, when there was no Opera House here at all. Where was I?"

"Your mother speaking German."

"Oh yes. Apparently, that is, it's not something that I know, I've just been told this by a doctor who saw my mother, your first language remains pretty much intact but you tend to lose a lot of any language you acquired later. It's a wonder that mum can still understand and speak English at all. But she's, I mean, she was a clever lady. It was mum who got my father hooked on books. Before then he was a man of action, you know, strike first, think later."

I knew that about her father. In fact I knew that better than she did.

"Is your father all right? He hasn't been making his usual visits to the home."

"I think so. He said he was troubled by something."

"Troubled? He doesn't have a job or anything, does he? What could be troubling him?"

"No, he hasn't had a job since he cashed out of his stocks in the computer business a decade ago."

"Was he in computers? I didn't know that."

"Oh yes. My father was trained by a colleague who also went to the United States. They had known each other at home in, uh, Switzerland, you know, and re-met in California. The colleague, whose name was Gustav—I called him 'Onkel Gustav'—had done a PhD at Caltech and took my father under his wing, getting him a job at IBM. Dad's drive took care of everything after that. He became an American and everything. He transferred to IBM here in Sydney and, well, that's how we got here. I think dad liked it here, I mean, the tranquility, the safe distance from, you know, from the turmoil."

"Turmoil? What do you mean?"

"Well, you know, in Europe and America everyone is either at each other's throats or, if not, at their feet. Australia is kind of in between. No one cares enough to bother you. They live their life and let you live yours."

We strolled along the paths that wound through the Botanical Gardens until we came to a statue of a boy convict. The boy was sitting on a stone bench with his crossed hands thrust deep into his jacket and his bare right foot, with toes curled, covering his left foot. It struck me as bizarre in that sweltering heat that this poor little boy, brought to this country against his will, was to be forever frozen in this cold and destitute pose in such a bright and bountiful garden.

I hadn't wanted to appear too insistent, so had waited some moments before questioning her further.

"You said he was troubled. By what? Am I prying?"

"Oh, no," she said, stopping under another Moreton Bay fig tree with its octopus-tentacle roots exposed around it. "Well, to tell you the truth, Liv ..."

She paused, suddenly looking straight into my eyes.

"Look, let's drop it," I said. "It's really none of my business.

Aren't these roots amazing...."

"Well, apparently it is," she said.

"It is what?"

"Your business."

"How so? What do you mean?"

"My father is being troubled, it seems, by you."

"By me? Why ever for?"

"Karen contacted him and asked him if he was German, not Swiss. She told him you said as much."

"Oh ... that!" I said with a shallow laugh. "No, that was just something, a kind of stupid coincidence, that I unearthed at the library. It's nothing. Forget it. I mean, tell her to forget it."

I started to walk ahead, but she called out to me from behind.

"My father was upset by this, Liv! He doesn't understand why you are doing what you are doing. That's why he visited me yesterday."

"What I'm doing? I'm not doing anything," I said, returning to where she was standing. "I just, you know, help care for his wife, I mean, your mother. I brought it up with Karen in all innocence. Really, in all innocence."

"Is that true, Liv? What are you trying to, I mean ..."

I interrupted her.

"Trying? I'm not trying," I said brusquely. "I said, I was just doing some research, that's all."

"Okay, okay," she said, putting her hand on my shoulder. "Just leave my father and me out of this. My mother, as you well know, is not long for this world."

"No, I didn't know that."

"She had cancer two years ago and went through the whole business. Her doctor said that they couldn't get at all of the tumour in her brain. It's growing, slowly, but growing."

"I thought she had senile dementia."

"She does. But it was brought on by the tumour. I really

don't understand these things very well. At any rate, we are taking her out of the home in the new year."

"Where will she go?"

"Home. My father is going to look after her. He's a saint … sometimes, that is, oh, not always. He was a terror when I was little. But he always did whatever he did out of love. To my father love is an absolute. There's no two ways about it. That's what he always says, and that's how he has lived his life. So, Liv, leave him alone, will you? He's an old man now. He's made his amends."

Those words of hers—that her father had "made his amends"—kept reverberating in my ears as I made my way back to my home. What did she mean? Was she acknowledging that her father had once committed atrocities against innocent people? Or was she just alluding to the way he brought her up, with a strictness that, in the end, dealt her more good than harm?

That night Karen phoned me. She was furious.

"What lies are you spreading about my grandfather?" she said. "What are you doing? Stan thinks you're really weird and that you have some kind of hidden agenda."

"What do you mean by 'agenda'? I don't understand."

"No, Liv, I think you do understand. Something you are hoping to get out of my family. Are you after money or something? Just leave us bloody alone, will you? What you are doing is evil. I'm sorry but I really think that. You have no right making up lies about people in my family. It hurts people. I spoke with my mother a couple of hours ago. She said you were trying to force information out of her. My mother may look okay but she's not well, you know. She had ovarian cancer and is not long out of the hospital. My grandfather is so worried about her. So just back off, okay?"

I made some sort of weak apology, assuring her that I was not trying to prove anything. She said one final word—

"Fine"—and hung up. I was unable to fall asleep that night. Had this obsession with Donald Meissner turned me into a hateful person, someone who puts on airs of charity and concern in order to uncover some vicious truth about another person, a truth that may or may not apply to him? No, this was no empty obsession. *That man* had committed crime after crime and, despite his past, he is living free while I, despite living a blameless life, have been bound to the past, unable to unlink the chains of memory for his constant presence in my mind. Now his daughter had truly confirmed my suspicions. His "amends"? A man cannot make his amends when he has not yet paid for his crimes, when he will not admit to himself and the world who he was and what he did to other people. I would put a life-size mirror in front of *that man*. Once he saw his true self in it I would let him go. I am not a vindictive person. I merely have a keen sense of justice.

Tokyo in the winter of 1945 was the calmest the city had been in years. The lifting of the fear of bombs and fire, the knowledge that you could sleep at night without being struck every hour and minute with sheer anxiety, gave the people of the city a deep sense of comfort. Despite the poverty and rampant disease, the shortage of shelter and the chaos of men and women moving aimlessly from one place to another, most people could finally go about their lives.

I was fortunate. Thanks to my language skills, I was hired on a casual basis by the allied occupation forces and put into a small team of interpreters and translators directly under Lt. Col. Charles Kades. I remember well the first time I met him in late November 1945.

"It says here that you worked in the German embassy."

"Yes. I was a translator there."

"From German? Or into German?"

"No. My German is not good enough for that. From Japanese to English. My, um, coworker and I provided information to the ambassador that originated in Britain or the U.S. and places."

"Intelligence."

"Yes. I suppose you could say so."

"Norwegian, eh?"

"Yes, sir."

"The wife and I went there on our honeymoon. Telemark. Beautiful. Remarkable people."

"Thank you. Actually, it may sound strange, but I have barely been in my country. I've spent my life in Japan. My parents were missionaries. Is that a problem?"

"Your parents being missionaries?" he said, peering at me over the rim of his glasses.

"No. My being in Japan without being Japanese."

"Nope. Fine by me. Character comes before country. Look, I'm sure you'll be fine. Start work tomorrow here in the embassy. I'll arrange a pass for you. Do you have accommodations, a place for yourself to stay? I mean, a woman in, uh, the family way."

"Um, yes. I lived in Tokyo up till April. The place where we lived survived the bombing and no one's come back there. Our stuff was still there when I returned recently."

"Got out while the getting was good, eh?"

He smiled at me, rose from his chair and shook my hand across his desk. He hadn't seemed to notice that I had said "the place where we lived" and referred to "our stuff" … or, if he had noticed, he was too polite to show it.

It was a few weeks later that I found out what happened to the staff at the German embassy. The lower-ranking workers were repatriated to Germany in September and October. Ambassador Heinrich Stahmer and Donald Meissner, who had been living in the hotel in Hakone, had undergone interrogation by the Japanese police. After the surrender on August 15th and the arrival of American forces the next month, the ambassador was sent home to Germany. I subsequently heard that he became a successful businessman, thanks to his close ties to the Japanese officials who had prosecuted the war. They had used their old connections to reinstate themselves in the world of commerce. Stahmer profited from his wartime associations.

"Donald Meissner is what we call a 'valuable asset,'" said Lt. Col. Kades when I met him before leaving for Norway.

"Asset?"

"Yes. He was the cleverest of the bunch. Our boys knew that even long before the war ended. They had their dibs on him. The Soviets got their Nazis and we got ours. One thing is for sure. Meissner was one lucky stiff. Had he gone back to Germany right after the war he wouldn't have fared well. The Germans are their own harshest critics. Meissner's already gone stateside. He'll be living the life of Riley before you know it. God bless America."

"Goodbye, Colonel Kades," I said, taking his hand and holding it in mine.

"You're a lovely girl, Liv. *Ha det bra* (Take care of yourself)."

I was moved to tears by his words. I had never heard a foreigner speak Norwegian. In fact I had not heard a single word of Norwegian—my native language—since my parents died in 1939.

Events of the next day revealed everything.

I had gone to the nursing home earlier than usual. Knowing then that Margaret Miles was dying made me feel that I had to show her as much kindness and warmth as possible in what were her last weeks at the home.

An enormous Christmas tree had been placed in the corner

along from the French doors. Nurse Victoria was standing on a stepladder decorating its branches with tinsel. It was an even hotter day than the previous day when I had strolled through the Botanical Gardens with Marlis Ditzen. The residents were sitting around in a circle awaiting the arrival of the man who played the guitar. Only Margaret was in her armchair by the window.

"Good morning, Margaret," I said, pulling up a chair and sitting beside her. "How are you today?"

"Fine, thank you."

"I'm Liv."

I showed her my name on the badge pinned to my dress.

"Yes, I know," she replied gruffly, turning her gaze to the window.

At that moment her husband arrived. He was dressed in crumpled tan trousers and a white shirt blotched with sweat. He wore no hat. He hobbled with his stick over to where we were sitting. He looked much more haggard than I had ever seen him. He pulled up the chair that was below the window and sat in it, taking his wife's hand in his.

"How are you, my dear?" he asked.

"Fine, thank you," she said, not taking her eyes off the tall eucalyptus tree in the garden beside the home.

He ignored my presence entirely. I may as well not have been there. He stroked her wrinkled hand and, as he did, dropped his stick to the floor. I bent over to pick it up, but he said "Leave it" without looking at me. He began to whisper something in German to her. As the whispers got progressively louder I could tell that he was singing to her. It was an old children's song I had heard before, one that Martin had sung to me in bed—*Kommt ein Vogel geflogen.*

A bird came flying
And sat on my foot.

In its beak there was a note
A greeting from my mother.

Dear bird, fly back!
Take my greeting with a kiss.
I cannot go with you
For I must stay here.

Margaret Miles, still staring at the tree, had tears in her eyes. I quietly rose and left them alone. He sat with her for over an hour, singing and talking to her in German, before slumping in his chair and falling asleep. His wife too slept, with her chin resting on her chest.

It was nearing noon when he awoke with a start, looked around, picked up his stick and stood up. He caught my eye as I was placing a lunch tray on a little table in front of one of the residents. He walked towards me, stopped, put the tip of his stick on the floor between his legs and, leaning on it, said, "I want to talk with you. Will you accompany me?"

I nodded, went to the office to tell Mrs. Archibold that I would be back after lunch, and left the home with him.

"Do you mind if we go to my apartment in Killara," he asked as we walked in the scorching heat up the hill towards the station.

"No. That's fine," I said.

We did not speak another word to each other until we reached the front door of his flat.

"I will open the door," he said, reaching into his trouser pocket for the key. "I have nothing to eat for you. I am sorry."

"I'm not hungry."

He opened the door and gestured for me to go in. I stepped into the living room. It was clean and tidy, furnished with light maple chairs and table. A television sat on top of a birch sideboard that looked Scandinavian in design.

"I will bring some tea, unless you prefer coffee."

"No, tea is fine, thank you."

He disappeared into the kitchen. I looked around the room. There were three oil paintings of European town scenes on the wall and, beside one of them, a photograph of two men. I sat for a few moments until my curiosity got the better of me and I walked over to the photograph. It showed him standing beside an older man at the foot of an enormous rock mountain. I unhooked the photograph and examined the faces of the two men closely, then replaced it on the wall. He came back into the room with a tray and glanced at the photograph, noticing that I had hung it on a slight angle.

"It was taken at Yosemite," he said, placing the tray on the table. On it were a pot of tea under an embroidered cosy, two pale-blue and white Meissen cups and saucers and a small plate of what looked like shortbread cookies. "It's me as a younger man. Well, I was already about fifty. The other person is a man who, you might say, saved my life. He gave me a new life. Los Angeles was a wonderful place in those days, the late 1940s and early fifties. Tens of thousands of people were pouring into the city from Iowa and Utah and Kansas. If you went to a park you saw more people having picnics there from some small town in the Midwest than had remained in the towns themselves. We were all determined to live a new life, so to speak, forget where we came from, even the Americans. Blot out the slate, toss it into the sea and go on from there, you know."

"Was that your colleague, the one from Caltech, in the photo?"

"Ah, yes, I have no secrets from you, do I. Yes, Gustav. Gustav Wagner. He was a man who didn't have a mean bone in his body. Milk? Sugar?"

"No thank you."

"Well, have a biscuit please. Genuine Scottish shortbread. A man has everything he needs here in Sydney."

"Thank you. No."

"So, Miss Grimstad, was it?"

"Yes."

"You seem to be doing some sort of research. Is it on me? Are you writing a novel? Or is this some sort of private detective work you dreamed up?"

I did not know what my next move should be. He was being so suave and polite. Not that Donald Meissner could not be suave and polite when such a pose allowed him to close in on his victim.

"May I ask you a question?" I said, after a moment of silence.

"Of course. You don't mind if I dip my biscuit in the tea, do you? Barbaric custom, but quite comforting. One of the few things I picked up from the Americans. So, what is your question?"

"Why did you bring me here, to your flat?"

"Well, you wanted to come, didn't you? You came here once, well, not into my flat, as you say. Mrs. Barnes told me. You also contacted my granddaughter and asked her to meet you in the city. You went all the way to the hospital to see my daughter, who was barely off the operating table after major surgery. You went so far as to tell the nurse there that you are my daughter. Who are you, anyway? Have you found out something that I do not know, perhaps that you *are* my daughter, a daughter I did not know I had? What are you trying to prove, Miss Grimstad?"

"Well," I said, putting my cup in the saucer and wiping my lips with the cloth napkin that was beside it. "I believe you are not the man you say you are."

He stared at me for a long time without saying a word. Then he rose, sighing deeply, and walked in shuffling steps to the photograph on the wall, taking it down and bringing it to me.

"This man ... *this man* ... was a Christlike figure. Are you religious yourself, Miss Grimstad?"

"No I'm not. But my parents were missionaries."

"Lutherans, of course."

"Yes, of course."

"Yes, yes. This man, Gustav Wagner, taught me that you can live out your life, even the final moments of your life, as a good person."

"Did he convert you?"

He burst out laughing.

"Convert? God no. I'm an atheist, Miss Grimstad. I have been since childhood. God never had much use for me, that's for sure. But my dear departed friend Gustav Wagner taught me that you can embrace whatever evil there is inside you. You don't need to pretend that it wasn't or isn't there. You hold it tight, contain it and make it your friend. The goodness in you cancels out the evil, or at least keeps it at bay. Goodness can be a shield, Miss Grimstad. It doesn't make you a good person in the end, but it makes you a tolerable one."

"Is that why you changed your name from Donald Meissner to Daniel Miles?"

"I beg your pardon?"

"Your name. The initials are the same."

"Initials? What does that tell you? The initials of the man who was my saviour were GW, the same as the initials of the man who is, or was, prime minister of this country. A sheer coincidence. What do such coincidences tell you? Just that there are many people in this world who seem to be alike, both the good and the bad. Am I like a man you once knew? It is often not so easy to distinguish between the two, Miss Grimstad."

"But your uncle, or whoever he was, the man at the department store in Berlin. He had the name Meissner. Is that a coincidence too?"

He rose again and walked towards the sideboard. But he suddenly grabbed his left wrist in his right hand and stumbled, dropping the photograph and smashing its glass. He looked down at the broken glass, steadying himself by gripping the protruding top of the sideboard.

"I'm sorry," I said.

"I must sit down," he said, easing himself into the upholstered chair next to the sideboard. "Why don't you leave me in peace? Why don't you?"

"Martin died, you know. It was because of the beatings. You put him there to save your skin."

He stared at me for well over a minute, shaking his head almost imperceptibly. Then he exhaled once, leaving his lips open. His expression froze like that. It was as if that exhalation was a last breath, as if he had expired before me. Finally he spoke in a whisper.

"I … I didn't beat him. The Japanese did."

"But you denounced him to them. Martin and I would have left together and been safe if you hadn't denounced him. We would have left you in peace then, Herr Meissner."

"It was better than denouncing him to the Germans. Had I done that, he would have been transported back to Germany and shot. At least … at least you got him back."

"You did it to save yourself!" I shouted. "You are living on his time!"

"Yes, you are right, Miss Bang. I did it to save myself. To save my own skin, as you rightfully say. This skin," he said, placing the palm of his right hand on the wrinkled skin of his left arm and stroking it.

His saying my name struck me like the blade of a knife, and I instinctively put my hands to my neck, breathing in and out as if panting. For thirty years I had thought about *that man*, and now he was sitting before me feeble, weak and, for the first time, vulnerable to me. I had never held power over anyone in my life. I had always been swayed by the power and mercy of others.

"I knew the moment I saw you on the train that it was you," he said. "I thought that you would not recognize me. I had my appearance altered in Los Angeles. They have the world's best cosmetic surgeons in that city. You cannot imagine what half the movie stars looked like before they arrived there. The Americans gave me a new Swiss birth certificate and passport. Then it was only a matter of changing the Swiss identity they created for me for an American one. I'm an American now. A true-blue American, as they say. There were Americans in intelligence, my wartime counterparts, whose actions caused the elimination of many more good people than mine did, you know. We all did things we despised ourselves for. We all did. I changed everything. I changed myself. Cannot a man have a new face to show the world? Is there no such thing as a new man?"

"You don't need to pay, then?"

"Pay?"

"Yes, pay! Not only Martin. All of the Jews and homosexuals you exposed and persecuted in Germany before you arrived in Japan, and the good Germans you denounced in Tokyo. Do their lives not matter to you? I lost the man I loved, Herr Meissner, and a baby!"

"Oh my God," he said, putting his head in his hands. He looked up at me with tears in his eyes. "Did I take away your baby from you too?"

I would not take my eyes off of him.

"Does your family know?" I asked.

"Margaret knows nothing anymore. She is the only one truly freed from the past. Marlis, of course, knows. She was nearly ten when we left Germany for Japan. She remembers Berlin well, and fondly, I might add. Why not? She was just a little girl. Karen doesn't know, or at least she didn't know until now. But she believes you. You have been very convincing with your 'research,' as you call it. I will tell her everything now, down to the last awful detail. Bravo, Liv Bang. You broke me. Bravo. I think we have finally managed to pass over the tail of the dog now, don't you? Is the war over now for you? Will it now go to someone else's threshold, another Liv Bang, another ... Donald Meissner. Dear me, I haven't said that name in nearly thirty years."

He tried to stand but seemed too weak to do so. For a moment he stared into his palms, then spoke again.

"I had tightly embraced Donald Meissner inside me and kept him at bay, and now you have brought that man back to life and freed him, here so far away from the life he led and many decades later. And for what? For who? Did you do this for yourself, to find the person inside you that you once were? If so, I hope to God that you found her and can go back to her. If I have accomplished something for you, it may be that. Now, please leave. Go. If you ever need me again, you'll now know where you can find me. I will speak and do as you say. But for now, please go. Please go. Please leave me in ...."

He left the last word unsaid, knelt by the legs of the chair and started to pick up the broken glass from the carpet, one piece after the other.

I recall a beautiful autumn day in Tokyo. What was the year? Perhaps it was 1943. Yes. Early November 1943. It was before Martin and I had become intimate. But even before then Inomata-san could tell that something was in the air.

We were sitting in our room on the second floor of the embassy, joking about where we would all end up. "I'll end up in my home village in Fukui. I can always go back to the land, even if life in the cities doesn't return to normal. My people were farmers. Of *kudzu*. Oh dear, the English word escapes me. Liv?"

"Is it arrowroot?" I said. "Something like that."

"Doesn't sound very attractive in either language. But you can do anything with *kudzu* ... make noodles out of it, a jelly, flour, sweet topping for desserts, anything. It's even good for a hangover, Martin."

"Don't look at me!" he said.

"If the land fails me at home, I'll just make my way to nearby Eiheiji Temple and sit Zen, staring at a wall with my legs crossed for the rest of my life. A wall is not a mirror, but it can have the same effect."

"Staring at a wall and looking at yourself ... sounds like a lifelong hangover," said Martin.

We all laughed.

"But, ah, you two. You two!" he said, standing between us. "You are destined for something wonderful. This war will end and gradually become part of the watercolour past. Maybe you will get married?"

"Inomata-san!" I exclaimed.

"Just imagining, Liv-san. Grant an old man his imagination. It may be the only free thing he has left. You'll get married and have lots of children. And you'll live happily ever after. Isn't that what it says in those fairy tales you have in your countries? At the very end?"

On Christmas Day I was phoned by Marlis Ditzen.

"Is that Liv?"

"Yes."

"It's Marlis."

"Oh. I meant to phone you. I do owe you an apology for the way I did things. Can we meet to talk? I really need to talk with you."

"I'm afraid I have some sad news for you."

I could tell by the tone of her voice that someone had died. It was no doubt her mother. I hadn't been at the home since visiting her father at his flat.

"My father is dead," she said.

"What?"

"He passed away last night."

"Oh."

That was all I could say. There was a long silence.

"He always had a weak heart. But in the end he took his own life, Liv. He slashed his wrists with some glass, sat in the bathtub and bled to death. No one knew. I had to go back into hospital for some tests and Karen is uncontactable. I think she might have already left for Europe with her boyfriend. … Hello? Are you there?"

"Yes, I'm here."

"We are holding a small service for my father at St. John's Church in Gordon on New Year's Eve at four in the afternoon. Will you come?"

"I really don't think your father would have wanted me to be there," I answered after a long pause.

"That's not true, actually. He left a note. Sorry, I'm getting choked up."

"Sorry. Take your time."

"He, uh, he left a note … to me and Karen. At the end of the note he wrote that he wanted to have a memorial service at the church and to especially ask you if you would attend."

"He did?"

"Sorry. It's still hard for me to speak. It's such a loss for me and our family. Yes. Please come, Liv. Please come. He wanted that."

It was only twenty-six degrees on the last day of 1975. The heat spell had broken. I had gone to David Jones on Boxing Day and had bought a black dress and a pair of patent leather pumps. I polished my grandmother's silver brooch until it shined and pinned it on my dress. The bright spoons dangled like little bells. I had never met my maternal grandmother, who had died in the year I was born, 1920. I had never even seen a photograph of her. Our people were too poor to own anything like a camera. The brooch was all I had to remind me of my Norwegian ancestry.

I arrived at the church just before four. Margaret was seated in the front row between Marlis and Mrs. Archibold. Nurse Victoria sat behind them. Across the aisle were Mr. and Mrs. Barnes and the young couple with their daughter who were his neighbours in the block of flats. In the back rows sat several groups of people of varying ages, but I had no way of knowing what connection they had with him. I walked up the aisle and sat beside Marlis, who nodded to me and smiled without parting her lips. Margaret noticed my presence and exclaimed in a boisterous voice, "Oh hello there!" Marlis put her finger to her lips and said, "Shush, mum."

The pastor, a handsome blond man with clear skin in his early thirties, appeared and stood at the lectern, in front of which was an open coffin with him in it. I could see from where I was sitting that his eyes were closed. Now he really did look like someone else.

"Welcome, everyone, and thank you for coming on this, the last day of the year. From tomorrow it's 1976 and we start the countdown to the 21st century. But since prophecy is not my forte, I will refrain from making a comment about what the future will hold for us here in Australia and for people around the world.

"My name is Martin Ulmer and I'm a Lutheran pastor. This is, of course, an Anglican church, but I have been assured by the pastor here that God turns a blind eye to all territorial issues. There's no geography in Heaven, you see, and the music you hear there will be played on any instrument your heart desires ... or your convictions demand.

"I was, for seven years, an army chaplain, and I can tell you that I have represented every religion and non-religion under the sun for many different kinds of people. According to Rabbi Esterowitz, who took over from me in Vietnam, I was the best teller of Jewish jokes this side of the Equator.

"Now, the deceased was a man I knew moderately well, though he was not one of my parishioners. We met by chance, actually, on a train going into the city. He taught me a great deal about the world and what makes people tick. And he was an avowed atheist. But if a Lutheran pastor can tell Jewish jokes, then an atheist can be a person with a profound conscience. It may pain us people of the cloth to admit it, but it's true. I remember a word he repeated to me. It's a German word. It is *Seelenfrieden*. Oh, do pardon my pronunciation. He said that it meant 'peace of mind,' but that literally it was 'peace for the soul.' He said that his heart occupied all regions of sorrow, and that he felt at rest only when, alone, he found himself surrounded by dark. He said, 'Martin, being able to see absolute darkness is perhaps the only saving grace of my life. I have found some very little light for myself in that darkness and some freedom here in Australia, the freedom to be kind to others for no reason whatsoever.' Then he confessed to me ... 'but I have not found peace for my soul.' I disagreed with him, but he just shook his head and hugged me tightly, very tightly, without letting go, in the very way my father used to do."

He paused for a moment to pour a glass of water for himself from a carafe on the lectern. He was obviously holding back tears.

"Has someone died?" asked Margaret, shaking her head back and forth as if not sure whether to ask the woman on her left or the woman on her right.

"*Das ist dein Mann, Mutter, dein Mann, Donald Meissner. Er ist tot.* (That is your husband, mother, your husband, Donald Meissner. He's dead)," said Marlis, with tears streaming down her cheeks, pointing to the man in the coffin.

"Oh," said Margaret, looking distressingly towards Marlis

and gripping Mrs. Archibold's hand until her knuckles turned white.

Then she leaned forward and stared at me. She must have recognized me as someone who had cared for her. She sat back, sighed deeply, shut her eyes and asked me in a whisper …

"Am I going home now?"

Lightning Source UK Ltd.
Milton Keynes UK
UKOW04f1422040218
317337UK00001B/62/P

9 781911 221272